JPB GOL
Time Will Tell

ROBIN JONES GUNN

BETHANY HOUSE PUBLISHERS
MINNEAPOLIS, MINNESOTA 55438

Time Will Tell
Copyright © 1998
Robin Jones Gunn

Edited by Janet Kobobel Grant

Cover design by Praco, Ltd. Cover illustration by George Angelini.

Published by Bethany House Publishers
A Ministry of Bethany Fellowship International
11300 Hampshire Avenue South, Minneapolis, Minnesota 55438

Printed in the United States of America by
Bethany Press International, Minneapolis, Minnesota 55438

Library of Congress Cataloging-in-Publication Data

Gunn, Robin Jones, 1955–
    Time will tell / Robin Jones Gunn.
        p. cm. — (The Sierra Jensen series ; #8)
    Summary: Faced with a serious lack of communication with her friend Amy, Sierra tries to trust in God to help her understand her relationships with others, including Paul, who has been sending her letters from Scotland.
    ISBN 1–56179–568–2
    [1. Friendship—Fiction. 2. Interpersonal relations—Fiction. 3. Family life—Fiction. 4. Christian life—Fiction.] I. Title. II. Series: Gunn, Robin Jones, 1955–   Sierra Jensen series ; #8.
PZ7.G972Ti 1998
[Fic]—dc21   97–51662
                                                     CIP
                                                     AC

98 99 00 01 02 03 04 / 12 11 10 9 8 7 6 5 4 3 2 1

To my "secret sisters" of One Heart:

May we always glorify the Lord and

be knit together in the unity of His Spirit.

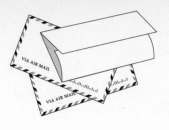

chapter one

*S*IERRA STOOD IN THE PARKING LOT AND NERVOUSLY nibbled on her thumbnail. She felt chilled in her shorts, T-shirt, and sandals. Leaning against her friend Amy's old Volvo, she waited for the back door of the restaurant to open.

Amy usually got off at eight. Sierra checked her watch: Eight-twenty. Where was Amy?

Gathering her courage, Sierra made her way to the front door of the Italian restaurant and opened it cautiously. She had planned that Amy would come to the parking lot and they could sit in her car to talk things through calmly. The last thing Sierra wanted was a confrontation in the lobby of Amy's uncle's restaurant.

Glancing around, Sierra noticed Amy wasn't at her usual spot behind the hostess podium. No customers were waiting to be seated. It was quiet. Exactly what Sierra had expected for a week night in September. That's why she had been certain Amy would get off at eight.

Sierra's buddy, Randy, was busing tables near the

hostess station. Sierra sneaked up behind him, leaned over, and said, "Boo!"

Randy turned around, his crooked grin proving that her shock tactics had no effect on his composure. "What's up?" he asked.

"I was hoping to catch Amy. Do you know if she has left?"

"She and Nathan left together. I think he said they were going down to The Beet."

The Beet was a new teen club that had opened that summer in downtown Portland. It featured local bands and served only nonalcoholic beverages. Sierra had heard all about it the first week of school from Randy and the other guys in his band. They were on the alternate list for October, which meant their band had a slight chance to make their big debut.

"I didn't see them come through the parking lot," Sierra said.

"They left through the front door. They're probably going to walk over. All the free parking near The Beet is taken by this time of night."

"Oh," Sierra said quietly.

"How long have you been waiting?"

"About half an hour."

Randy gave her a sympathetic look. "You and Amy haven't talked yet?"

Sierra shook her head. "I've tried. All week at school she had someone else to talk to or someplace to go right after class. I've called her, I've left notes in her locker, and now . . ."

"And now you're waiting for her in the parking lot," Randy said, shaking his head.

His straight blond hair had grown out over the summer, and he had to wear it pulled back in a short ponytail when he worked. He had already received a notice at the private Christian high school they attended advising him that his hair exceeded the acceptable length as stated on page 14 of the Royal Academy Student Handbook.

"I know. You think I'm pathetic, the way I'm stalking her," Sierra said. "It's just that I'm not ready for our friendship to be over until we at least have a chance to talk about it."

"And Amy doesn't feel that way," Randy surmised.

Sierra shook her head and her turquoise-beaded earrings brushed her jawline.

"Don't give up," Randy said, giving her a quick squeeze on the shoulder. "Remind yourself of that verse you kept telling me when you got back from Switzerland." Randy seemed to have suddenly lost his memory. He looked at Sierra. "What was it you kept saying?"

"Love each other deeply, because love covers over a multitude of sins." Sierra recited the verse like a bored kid at vacation Bible school.

"That's the one. Keep telling yourself to love Amy like that. She'll come around."

Sierra sighed. "I don't know."

An older couple got up from their table, and Sierra moved to let them pass.

"I'd better let you get back to work," she said.

"Okay. I'll see you tomorrow at school," Randy said,

heading for the table the couple had just vacated.

Sierra slipped out of the restaurant as quietly as she had slipped in. She climbed into her car and drove home with the windows rolled up and the heater on. It was too cold for this time of year, especially when it still looked like summer all around. Sierra wasn't ready for summer to be over. Without a doubt, this had been her best summer yet, full of travel, friends, adventure, and even a little brush with romance. In the same way she wasn't ready for summer to end, she knew she wasn't ready for her friendship with Amy to be over.

It had been a simple misunderstanding. Amy had taken an interest in Nathan when he came to work at her uncle's restaurant at the beginning of the summer. Nathan asked Amy out, and when she called to give Sierra an account of their first date, Sierra had jumped all over Amy for making out with Nathan in his car. Amy had hung up, and since then they had spoken no more than a few sentences to each other.

Sierra was gone for several weeks, and when she came back, it was a mad rush to get everything ready for school. It had been almost five weeks now since Sierra and Amy had talked, and from the looks of things, Amy and Nathan were still very much together.

Pulling into the narrow driveway of her family's old Victorian home, Sierra turned off the engine in the 1979 VW Rabbit her parents had given her the week before. It was a mixed blessing to have her own car. Last year she had shared the Rabbit with her mom, which meant her dad paid for her insurance. Now that it was her car, the insurance bill was hers also. As long as she kept up her grades, her rate would stay the same, and her part-time job at Mama Bear's Bakery should cover her expenses. It didn't leave much money over for exciting adventures such as the one she had spent her savings on this past summer.

Sierra sat in the warm car a few minutes. *Is it me? Am I making too big of a deal out of this face-to-face with Amy? Should I let it go? I want to prove to her I really am her friend, no matter what. How can I prove that to her if she won't respond?*

Locking the car door, Sierra shuffled through the damp grass to the front porch, where the amber light glowed above the door, welcoming her home. Amy had once accused Sierra of having the perfect family and the perfect home. At this moment, it felt perfect. Her parents were still in love after 27 years of marriage. Granna Mae lived with them, or rather, they lived here with her—it was her house. And Sierra's four brothers and one sister were all living happy lives.

Sierra wiped her feet on the welcome mat before she went in. She thought back to when she had stood here a week and a half ago with tears streaming down her cheeks as her favorite brother, Wesley, had driven off to college in Corvallis in his fixed-up sports car. She loved her brother and had relied on him more than she realized this past summer.

Wes was the one she had told about Alex, the tall Russian she had met on her trip to Switzerland. Sierra also had confided in Wes about the letter she had received from Paul three weeks ago. Paul, her mysterious friend with the blue-gray eyes, was going to school in Scotland. She hadn't shown Wes the letter, but she did describe to him how Paul said he went hiking through the Highlands of Scotland, singing aloud to God. Wes hadn't laughed. Instead, he had folded his arms, nodded, and said, "Now there's a brave heart for you. Keep praying for that one, Sierra."

She had taken his advice and not only continued to pray for Paul but had also written him—twice. He hadn't written back.

As Sierra opened the front door, her mom poked her head around the corner from the kitchen. Sharon Jensen had a worried look on her face and the phone to her ear. She waved at Sierra with a flutter of her fingers.

Sierra headed for the study, her favorite room in the house. It was also her dad's office and Granna Mae's old library. Sierra liked to retreat there to do her homework and smell the mixed scent of leather and old books. She had left her backpack in the den that afternoon while doing homework. When she pushed open the door, she saw that her father was at the desk, also on the phone. He didn't look up when she came in.

Quietly gathering her textbooks and stuffing them into her pack, Sierra heard her dad say, "Okay, honey, we'll talk again in a few days. You do know that Mom and I support you in this decision, don't you? . . . Okay. . . . Good. Call us and let us know what you decide. . . . Bye-bye."

There were only three women Howard Jensen called "honey," and two of them were in this house at this moment. The other "honey" was Sierra's sister, Tawni, who had been living in Southern California for the past few months so she could be closer to her boyfriend, Jeremy. As her dad said good-bye and hung up the phone, Sierra began to feel a little nervous about Tawni.

"Is everything okay?" she asked when her dad turned to her.

"Tawni has a big decision ahead of her." Mr. Jensen's usually happy eyes were clouded over.

Just then Sierra's mom stepped into the den. She didn't notice Sierra sitting in the corner chair. "Oh, Howard, I don't know about this. What do you think?"

Mr. Jensen glanced at Sierra, and his wife followed his gaze.

Mrs. Jensen pursed her lips, working up a smile for Sierra. "I didn't see you there, Sierra. How did your time go with Amy?"

"We didn't talk," Sierra said. "She'd already left. I'll try again tomorrow, I guess."

"That sounds like a good idea."

Sierra could tell her mom wasn't thinking about Amy.

"Is Tawni all right?" Sierra asked tentatively.

"Yes," Mrs. Jensen stated, looking at her husband.

Neither of them offered any more information.

Rats! Sierra thought. *Something is going on, but they're not going to tell me. Is it something to do with Jeremy?*

Sierra glanced at the clock. She looked back at her parents and caught them sending each other the silent message *Don't say anything.*

"I'll get out of here," Sierra said. She felt like adding, "So you can have your big, private conversation about Tawni without me hanging around." But she held her tongue and slipped past them, closing the door behind her. She knew she should appreciate that her parents kept Tawni's situation confidential. If it had been she, Sierra would want to count on them to keep her news quiet.

Trudging up the stairs to her bedroom, Sierra muttered to herself, "This is so frustrating. All I can do is wait. Wait for another chance to talk to Amy. Wait for Paul to write. Wait to see if Mom and Dad will include me in Tawni's problem. Wait, wait, wait. I hate waiting."

Sierra opened her bedroom door and tossed her backpack into the corner by the closet. Her relaxed attitude about cleaning up expressed itself all over the room, making it hard for her to find a place to flop down and have a decent pout party. Sierra had to admit her room was a startling sight. Clothes, books, bags, socks, plates, CDs, hats, papers, and a crazy variety of "stuff" covered her large upstairs bedroom with no semblance of order. She could usually find what she wanted, and she believed more important and interesting things were to be done than sort and organize belongings.

If everything else in her life was on hold, Sierra decided she might as well add her room to the list. She would wait until tomorrow to clean it.

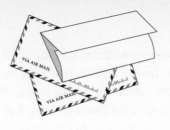

chapter two

OMORROW TURNED INTO THE NEXT DAY AND THE next until finally, on Friday night, Sierra was back in her room, trying to think of a way to make sense of the mess. The rest of her life was still in disarray. Her parents had answered her questions about Tawni by saying they would leave it up to Tawni to tell Sierra and her brothers. She knew then the decision couldn't be to get married or move back home or anything that radical because her parents wouldn't have hesitated to share that information with all of them.

Still no word had winged its way to her from Paul. Then there was elusive Amy, who kept disappearing down the hallway at school whenever Sierra tried to approach her.

Resigning herself to trying to do something about her room, Sierra set about the task. The exercise of picking up, sorting, and putting away helped restore order in more ways than one. As she stuffed clothes into her dresser drawers, she devised a plan for meeting with Amy. The next morning Sierra didn't have to be to work at Mama

Bear's until ten. She would take a picnic breakfast to Amy's and wake her up. They could sit on Amy's bed, eat breakfast, and have the heart-to-heart talk they needed. Amy couldn't walk away from Sierra in her own room.

Sierra smashed down the junk in her trash can and added another handful. She stacked her books on the floor beside her bed and smoothed back the comforter on top of Tawni's bed. Scooping up a huge armful of dirty clothes, Sierra made her way to the basement, where she started to feed all her dark-colored clothes into the gaping mouth of the washing machine. That was only the first load. She had hauled down enough for at least two more loads, which meant she would be up and down these stairs all night.

The basement's smell brought mixed memories. When Sierra was a child, this had been a great hiding place when her family came to visit Granna Mae. Once Sierra had wedged her skinny frame behind the stack of Christmas decoration boxes and pulled an old trash can filled with rakes and shovels beside her to close off the opening. For the first five minutes or so, she felt wonderfully sneaky. She smiled, hugging her knees to her chest and waiting for someone to come look for her.

Then the thrill wore off. The icy cement floor had turned her bottom numb, and the once-exotic swampy fragrance now stuffed up her nose and made her eyes itch. She had no room to stretch her cramping legs.

Unable to stay in hiding any longer, Sierra had pushed the trash can back herself, stood up, and shook her legs to make the tingles go away. Then slowly taking the stairs, she made her way to the front yard, where she found her sister and all four brothers huddled around a cardboard box from which a neighbor's six kittens mewed for attention.

Clicking on the washing machine and drawing her thoughts back to the present, Sierra remembered how at the time she didn't care about the kittens. She wanted to know why no one had come looking for her. Why hadn't they cared enough?

A smile came to her face as she remembered the way Tawni had begged their dad to let her keep one of the kittens. He had refused. Mr. Jensen was a dog man, not a cat man. Not even the helpless ball of caramel fur Tawni held up to his face, with tears in her eyes, changed his mind that summer afternoon. However, that Christmas, Tawni received an all-white kitten. She named it Snowflake, and it lived in a cozy bed beside the dryer.

Taking the basement stairs two at a time, Sierra left the musty smells and childhood memories behind. She decided to fix her breakfast picnic now while waiting for her laundry. Finding some bagels, she packed them in one of her mom's wicker baskets hanging on a peg in the kitchen. From the refrigerator, she took a tiny jar of blackberry jam from the door rack, two oranges from an open bowl on the shelf, and a couple of eggs marked with happy faces. The black pen faces were Mrs. Jensen's code for Sierra's younger brothers, Gavin and Dillon, to let them know which of the eggs were hard-boiled. Two years ago Gavin took what he said he thought was a hard-boiled egg and cracked it over Dillon's head. After all the boys' wailing and hollering, their mom had devised the happy face code.

Covering the now-full basket with a dish towel, Sierra felt pleased with her picnic and her plan. Just then her two younger brothers came in with their dad. They each had a miniature wooden car to show Sierra.

"I'm going to paint mine tomorrow," Gavin said. "Hot red so it'll go fastest."

"Those turned out nice," Sierra said, examining Dillon's car up close.

Both her brothers had entered a toy boxcar derby contest at the city park.

Mrs. Jensen stepped into the kitchen with a tray of dirty dinner dishes. "Granna Mae is already asleep. I think you boys need to head to bed now, too."

After the usual round of groans and complaints, the boys made their way up the stairs.

Mr. Jensen stepped into the entryway and called after them in a strong whisper, "Not so loud. Don't wake Granna Mae."

"What have you been doing all night?" Mrs. Jensen asked Sierra.

"Picking up my room a little."

Her mom's eyes seemed to brighten. "Really? Good for you."

"I have some laundry going, and I put together a breakfast picnic for tomorrow. I plan to go over to Amy's and wake her up."

"You two still haven't talked?"

"No. And it's hanging over me like an overdue term paper."

"I hope you settle it soon," her mom said, checking the

dishes in the dishwasher, trying to determine if they were dirty or clean. "Unresolved relationships can really wear a person out."

Mr. Jensen stepped back into the kitchen in time to pick up the last bit of their conversation. "You talking about Tawni?"

Mrs. Jensen and Sierra both turned to look at him. Mrs. Jensen's look said, *What are you doing?* while Sierra's begged, *Tell me more!*

"I guess not," Mr. Jensen said, reaching for a glass in the cupboard and pouring himself a drink of water. He sipped the water slowly, watching both of them over the top of the glass. Without offering any information, he placed the empty glass on the counter and, with a wry grin to his wife, said, "Carry on, then. As you were." With a mock salute, he headed out the back door to his workshop.

"Is there anything I should know about Tawni?" Sierra asked her mom after he left. "I mean, I already know she's trying to make a big decision, and now I can guess it has to do with a broken relationship. It isn't Jeremy, is it? She isn't going to break up with him, is she?"

Mrs. Jensen had concluded that the dishes were dirty and was trying to wedge in the last few glasses. She didn't say anything but worked silently, pouring the soap into the dispenser. As she clicked the knob to "On," her words seemed to come.

"I'm not sure what to say, honey. I think Tawni would prefer we not tell you until she's made her final decision. It'll only be a few days, and I think she would feel better about us doing it that way."

"But we're a family," Sierra said. "Why should families keep things from each other?"

Her mom sighed and leaned back against the counter, folding her arms across her middle. A frustrated look came over her face. "You're right. That's been our policy all along. We keep things open and honest in the Jensen clan. But I think it's better that we wait for Tawni to decide what she wants to do, and then we can all talk about it."

Sierra couldn't begin to imagine what would be so secretive. Returning to the basement to put her clothes in the dryer and start a new load, Sierra could only hope her sister's secret was something good. Maybe like her Christmas kitten. Maybe Tawni's news was something like that.

And then again . . .

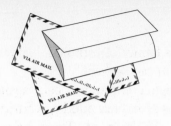

chapter three

*T*HE NEXT MORNING SIERRA DRESSED FOR WORK AND left at seven-thirty with her picnic basket. She drove to Amy's house with a prayer for peaceful reconciliation on her lips. Sierra rang the doorbell three times before Amy's groggy, grumpy father opened the door in his robe.

"Oh, I'm sorry I woke you up. I wanted to surprise Amy. I brought a breakfast picnic for us."

Mr. DeGrassi gave Sierra a baffled look.

"I'm Sierra. Sierra Jensen. I know I haven't been over for awhile . . ."

"Amy stayed at her mother's last night," Mr. DeGrassi said. Without any further explanation, he closed the door.

Sierra nearly dropped the basket. *At her mother's! What does he mean? Amy's mom moved out?*

Stumbling back to her car, Sierra realized how out of touch with Amy she had become. Earlier in the summer, Amy had confided in Sierra that her parents had been fighting and Amy had overheard them talking about divorce. Sierra had tried to convince Amy that it wasn't serious. All parents have misunderstandings. Everything would work out fine, she had told Amy. Obviously, Sierra had been wrong.

Stunned, she drove home. When she turned onto 52nd Street, she noticed Randy was mowing the lawn at one of his regular yard jobs. He had started his own lawn maintenance business in the spring and then took the part-time busboy position at the restaurant during the summer. With two jobs and all the hours he put into the band, which practiced three nights a week in Randy's garage, he had been busy all summer.

Sierra pulled up to the curb and parked the car. Taking the basket with her, she walked toward Randy, waving and calling his name. He wore an earphone, with the wire running to a cassette player clipped on the back of his jeans.

"Yo!" Sierra called out again, only a few feet away.

Randy looked up, shut off the lawn mower, and pulled out the earpiece. "Hey, what's up?" he asked.

"Did you know Amy's parents aren't together anymore?"

"Yes."

"Why didn't you tell me?"

"I thought everybody knew."

"I didn't know. I went over there this morning and found out from her dad. He didn't look too happy."

Randy looked at the basket. "What's that?"

"A picnic."

"Food?" Randy asked.

"I had this great idea to surprise Amy with a breakfast

picnic, only she stayed at her mom's last night. I can't believe this. How has Amy taken it all?"

"I don't know. At work she pretty much keeps to herself and then leaves with Nathan when she gets off. I think her mom moved into an apartment over on Halsey. I heard Amy telling someone at work a few weeks ago."

"When did all this happen?"

"While you were gone."

Sierra shook her head and sighed. "I feel awful for her."

Randy nodded and motioned toward the basket. "So, what's in the basket?"

"Why? You hungry?"

Randy's half-grin told her it was a pointless question. "Hot cinnamon rolls from Mama Bear's, I hope," Randy suggested.

"No, low-fat bagels. Sorry. I packed it for Amy and me."

"Bagels are good," Randy said, taking the basket from Sierra and leading her over to a part of the lawn he had already mowed. He sat down and pulled back the dish towel. "Do you have anything to drink?"

"No."

"I have some drinks in my truck." Randy sprang up and returned with two cans of cream soda. It didn't seem the likely beverage to accompany hard-boiled eggs and bagels, but Sierra didn't complain. She was just glad she had Randy to talk to. It seemed he was her only close friend.

"What do you want first?" Sierra asked. "The bagel or the egg?"

"Is this a variation on that age-old question: Which came first, the bagel or the egg?" Randy grinned at his own joke. "Give me both. I'll make a sandwich." He pulled out his pocketknife and wiped it on the leg of his jeans. Then he created a breakfast bagel.

Sierra looked around the quiet neighborhood as it began to wake up. "Do you think it's okay that we're sprawled out on these people's lawn?"

"Sure. They won't mind."

Sierra opened her bagel and spread it with the jam. Overhead she could hear doves cooing in the trees. A row of perky-faced pansies from the flower bed watched Randy and Sierra enjoy their morning feast. The pleasant, peaceful setting didn't match Sierra's emotions. She willed herself to downshift and enjoy this time with Randy, who was quite possibly her one and only true friend this school year. She knew one question that guaranteed to get him talking.

"So, how are things going with the band?"

"Vicki came to hear us practice last night," Randy said, snapping open the lid of his soda can. "She thinks we're sounding pretty good."

Sierra hadn't heard the band practice for weeks. She had sat in on a jam session once, but it drove her crazy to listen to the same piece of music over and over.

"That's good. Have you guys come up with a name yet that you can all agree on?"

"Almost."

"Do you mean the name of the band is 'Almost' or you've almost come up with a name?"

Randy chuckled. "I should throw that one into the mix.

'Almost.' That would be a pretty radical name. What I mean is that we almost had a name, but Ben was pretty sure it was already taken. It was 'White Horse.' Vicki said there was a way of checking it on the Internet, so she's going to find out for us."

"That's nice of her." Sierra thoughtfully chewed her bagel and swallowed her feelings about Vicki.

Last semester Vicki had asked Randy out to a formal benefit dinner, and Sierra had labeled her a flirt. Maybe it wasn't a fair assessment of Vicki, but the two of them had gotten off on the wrong foot when Sierra had moved to Portland. Sierra had overheard Vicki and another girl talking about her in the locker room Sierra's first week of school. The other girl said she thought Sierra was stuck up. Sierra had marched around to their side of the lockers, blasted out that she wasn't stuck up, and then marched out of the locker room.

Looking back, that seemed a ridiculous way to handle the situation. She had only proved they were right by overreacting. The unfortunate result was that Sierra had labeled Vicki then as someone to avoid. It hadn't helped a bit when Vicki asked Randy out. At that point, Sierra was just beginning to feel as though Randy was her close friend, and then Vicki seemed to be wiggling in between them.

At the end of the school year, Vicki had been assigned to the same special project team as Randy and Sierra when they helped out at the Highland House, a homeless shelter where Sierra still occasionally volunteered. Vicki hadn't exactly put her heart into the project. She hadn't even managed to show up most of the time.

Suddenly, Sierra felt an interest in listening to the band practice again. She knew it was crazy. She only wanted to hear the band because Vicki was hanging out with Sierra's friends and she didn't trust her.

Maybe if Vicki weren't so gorgeous, Sierra would have felt differently. Vicki's silky, light brown hair hung down her back. She wore it parted down the middle and was forever flipping it over her shoulders. Her thin, arched eyebrows framed her green eyes and gave her face a centered look. When a person looked at Vicki, the first thing he saw were her eyes.

Sierra felt inferior when she compared herself with Vicki. A person's first impression of Sierra, she imagined, would be her unruly hair. She knew she had nice eyes. They were a blue-gray color, and she had been told they seemed to change with the weather. Her figure had always been closer to a tomboy's than a beauty queen's, though Sierra had noticed this fall that some of her school clothes had gotten tighter on her: either she had shrunk everything in the wash or her body was actually launching into her final, late-bloomer stage of development. She hoped it was the latter.

Realizing she had been quiet for a long time, she wrapped up her private thoughts and asked Randy how the lawn-care business was. He didn't seem to have noticed how quiet she had been, since he had been busy eating.

"I've cut back some for the fall, but I think I'm going to have to quit my job at the restaurant. They scheduled me for 16 hours this week, but with school and the lawns, I don't have enough time for the band."

"Have you given your notice yet?"

"No, I was thinking and praying about it this morning. What do you think?"

"I think you can't do everything. Something has to go."

"I make more money on the lawns, and I can get them done if I work all day Saturday. That gives me week nights for the band."

"Sounds as if you could leave the restaurant and it wouldn't hurt your finances too much," Sierra said.

"I asked my parents last night, and they said it was up to me. They said they would support my decision, whatever I end up doing."

"Don't you hate that?" Sierra said. "I sometimes wish my parents would just tell me what to do instead of leaving it up to me."

"I know. Funny, isn't it? A few years ago I was complaining to my parents that they wouldn't give me enough freedom to make my own decisions. Now they are, and I'm complaining again."

Randy popped the last bite of his bagel into his mouth. A crumb of egg yolk clung to the corner of his lower lip. Sierra motioned for him to brush it away.

He wiped his mouth and said decidedly, "I'm going to give my notice this afternoon at the restaurant."

"How many more lawns do you have to do today?"

"Eight."

"Are they all as big as this one?"

Randy looked around. "Some. Some are smaller. I don't know. It takes about an hour at each house. Except some of the ones around here. They only take half an hour or so. I do 10 houses. Makes for a long Saturday, but like I said, the money is great."

"I'd better let you get back at it," Sierra said. "Thanks for sharing my little picnic with me."

"Anytime," Randy said with a smile. "It's too bad Amy wasn't at her dad's, but her loss was my gain." He patted his stomach contentedly.

Sierra gathered up the basket and drove to work. The bakery already had a line of customers inside when Sierra arrived. She washed her hands, put on her apron, and took over for Jody at the cash register. The soothing scent of freshly baked cinnamon rolls circled the bakery, enticing more customers to come inside every time the door opened and some of the aroma escaped.

Sierra knew she had a great job. She loved the people she worked with, especially Mrs. Kraus, who ran the bakery. She had understood when Sierra went to Southern California during the summer. Then when Sierra called to say she was going to be gone for another week because she had the chance to fly to Europe with her friend Christy, Mrs. Kraus had assured her not to worry about a thing. That short but meaningful jaunt to Switzerland and Germany had changed Sierra deep down, helping her to understand more about relationships and not to force them into boxes that didn't fit them. She didn't always apply that principle well, but she was trying. And Amy was one of the people with whom she wanted to try.

As Sierra cleaned out the coffee filter from the espresso machine, she noticed two customers running in the door, soaked from the sudden downpour of autumn rain. The shimmering wonder of summer had officially ended.

chapter four

*S*IERRA DIDN'T DISLIKE THE RAIN, BUT SHE DIDN'T LOVE it either. It was just something she lived with in Portland. Sometimes, when the gentle taps danced on her bedroom window, it had a soothing effect on her. Other times it meant a forced retreat from a softball game or from a walk with their Saint Bernard, Brutus.

When she finished work and drove home, Sierra went upstairs to her partially cleaned room, where she grabbed her favorite pair of jeans and one of Wesley's OSU sweatshirts, which she hadn't realized she had confiscated, and headed for the bathtub. It had been a long time since she had had a good soak.

As she rubbed the cinnamon roll and coffee fragrances from her skin, Sierra tried to think about nothing. She had checked the mail, but no letters had arrived from Paul. Big surprise. She didn't want to speculate anymore on Tawni's problem, and she was pretty discouraged about trying to talk to Amy.

Relationships are supposed to be two-way streets, aren't they? I'm not supposed to be the only one pursuing, am I?

She wasn't exactly sure if she was thinking about her relationship with Paul or with Amy. It didn't matter. They both seemed to be in the same mode: silence—like Tawni's unspoken decision.

Whoever said silence is golden obviously never had the kinds of friends and relatives I have.

Then, because it was much too quiet in the bathtub, Sierra cut short the soak and slipped into her bum-around-the-house clothes. She headed downstairs, looking forward to the noise and activity of her family.

She found her mom, Granna Mae, and Dillon in the kitchen. Mom was setting paper plates on the counter, and Dillon was checking his race car to see if the paint had dried.

"You might leave a fingerprint," Sierra warned. "It's better to let it stay on the paper towel until tomorrow."

Dillon looked as though he was having a hard time deciding if he should heed his sister's advice or go with his impulse. His impulse won. He looked around sheepishly to see if anyone had noticed. Sierra was still watching him.

"It's almost dry," Dillon said and then left the room, casually trying to rub the smudge of red off his fingertip.

"Caught red-handed," Sierra called out after him with a laugh.

"What was that?" Granna Mae asked, turning around from the sink where she was rinsing out a china cup.

"I was talking to Dillon, Granna Mae," Sierra said. "What's for dinner, Mom?"

"Dad went to get some Chinese food."

"Perfect," Sierra said, her mood beginning to pick up.

"Oh," Granna Mae said. Her face scrunched in disapproval. "I don't believe I'd like Chinese food. I'd prefer some soup." She headed for the pantry and asked over her shoulder, "Would anyone else like some?"

"No thanks," Sierra answered for them both.

"Here, let me do that for you, Granna Mae," Sierra's mom said.

"I can do this fine by myself, Sharon."

"But I'd like to help you, Mother."

Granna Mae turned and gave Sharon a bewildered look. "I'm not your mother, am I?"

"Your son, Howard, is my husband," Mrs. Jensen said calmly. "You're my mother-in-law."

"Yes, I know that." Now Granna Mae sounded irritated. She had a can of chicken and rice soup in her hand, which she plopped down on the counter. "And this is my house. All you people are here in my house, and you're trying to keep me from making myself some soup."

Mrs. Jensen backed off. Sierra knew that when Granna Mae got confused, it was better to say very little. However, Granna Mae didn't seem confused. Everything she said was true. This *was* her house. When it became apparent that she couldn't live here by herself, Sierra's large family had left Pineville in northern California and had moved in. It meant big adjustments for all of them. But never in the last year while they had lived here had Sierra heard Granna Mae declare this was her house, as if she needed to stake her claim.

"We're not trying to keep you from anything," Mrs. Jensen said calmly. "I thought maybe I could help."

"Help me to open a can of soup? I don't think I need help. In all my days, I've never needed help opening a can of soup."

Granna Mae continued to mutter as she fished out a can opener from the drawer. Poor Granna Mae couldn't get the can opener to catch on the lip of the can, a simple process for steady hands but an exasperating chore for someone with shaky ones. At last she got the opener to cooperate, and she turned the handle with great effort. Sierra wanted to step in and do it for her, but she knew it was better to let her grandmother do this herself.

With the can opened and the lid barely hanging on by a catch in the metal, Granna Mae bent over and hunted for a soup kettle. She pulled one out from the cupboard and dumped the soup in. Then she slowly turned the knob to light the gas flame. Sierra marveled at how difficult everything seemed to be for her grandmother.

As the soup heated up, Granna Mae returned to the pantry for a box of crackers. She took a bowl from the cupboard and a spoon from the drawer. She seemed to be in her own little world. Sierra didn't talk to her or try to help. Instead, she wiped the counter around the sink, the way she cleaned up at work, and chatted with her mom. But both of them were watching Granna Mae out of the corners of their eyes.

When the soup was bubbling, Granna Mae found a pot holder and carefully ladled the soup into her bowl. She carried the bowl to the dining room table, leaving Sierra and her mom alone in the kitchen. For the first time, Sierra began to understand the kind of pressure her mother had been under all these months as she lovingly cared for her mother-in-law, following her around the house and making sure she wasn't endangering herself or others. It was worse than when Dillon was a toddler. At least Dillon could be kept in a closed-off area. Granna Mae could open doors, turn on stove tops, and even possibly wander off someday.

"Is there anything I can do to help out?" Sierra asked.

"You mean with dinner?"

"No." Sierra lowered her voice. "With Granna Mae."

Her mom shrugged. "She's been doing pretty well lately."

"I know, but don't you have to keep an eye on her all the time?"

Her mom nodded.

"Why don't I do something like take her out for an afternoon so you don't have to think about her?"

"It's okay, Sierra. This is your senior year. You have a job. Your life is full already."

"There's room for my grandma in it," Sierra stated a little too loudly before lowering her voice again. "I'd like to do something."

Mr. Jensen and Gavin arrived just then with the tall white bags filled with boxes of Chinese food.

"Let's get this food on while it's still hot," Mr. Jensen said. "Gavin and I almost tore into it on the way home."

Mrs. Jensen reached for some serving spoons and said to Sierra, "It's fine with me if you arrange something. Make sure it's okay with Granna Mae first. She does better if she has time to think through any changes in her schedule."

Sierra went into the dining room, where Granna Mae

was rising from her chair. Sierra again resisted the urge to help her.

"Are you sure you don't want some Chinese food?" Sierra asked. "It smells really good."

"No, no. I'm fine. The soup is too hot, though. I thought I'd take it up to my room and let it cool."

"I'll take it for you," Sierra said, quickly reaching for the bowl before Granna Mae's shaky hands had a chance to lift it.

"Thank you, Lovey. I'd appreciate that."

Sierra suddenly breathed easier. It seemed that whenever Granna Mae was thinking clearly, she called Sierra "Lovey." It was to Sierra what the childhood call of "Olly, Olly, Oxen-free" used to mean when she played hide-and-seek. It meant the coast was clear. Come out of hiding. Everything is okay now.

Sierra followed her grandmother up the stairs, each step a greater effort to conquer for the woman than the last. Again, Sierra was overwhelmed with the thought of how hard everyday life was for her dear grandmother.

"Can I get you anything else?" Sierra asked after Granna Mae had settled herself in her recliner.

"No, no. This is lovely. Thank you." She smiled sweetly as if she were dismissing Sierra.

Heading downstairs, Sierra thought of how, when her family had first moved in, she had thought it unkind of her parents not to include Granna Mae in all the family's meals together. Now Sierra was beginning to understand. With the noise and activity that come with a big family, it was much more calming for Granna Mae to eat by herself in her large, comfy bedroom.

By the time Sierra returned to the kitchen, everyone had dished up and gathered around the dining room table. It was then that Sierra remembered she was going to ask Granna Mae about the two of them scheduling something to do. She would ask her later. Right now an alluring box of sweet-and-sour pork was calling to her.

Sierra scooped out the last of the pork, thankful that Dillon hadn't taken it all since that was his favorite. Sierra unwrapped a set of the wooden chopsticks and was about to pop the first tender morsel of pork into her mouth when the phone rang. With plate in hand, she picked up the receiver. It was her sister.

"Hey, Tawni," Sierra said, imitating Randy's usual greeting. "What's up?"

"A lot, actually," she said.

"I suppose you want to talk to Mom and Dad," Sierra said, balancing the portable phone on her shoulder and drawing the chopsticks full of sweet and sour pork to her mouth.

"Actually, I'm glad I caught you. I'd like to ask your opinion about something."

The meat tumbled from Sierra's chopsticks onto her plate. She put down her food and leaned against the counter, hardly daring to believe her own ears. Such words had never crossed her sister's lips.

"Sure," Sierra said, trying not to sound shocked or overly excited about being invited into the big decision. "What's going on?"

chapter five

"WHAT HAVE MOM AND DAD TOLD YOU?" Tawni asked.

"Nothing."

Tawni sighed into the phone. "Aren't they the best, Sierra?"

Now Sierra was completely lost. "The best what?"

"The best parents. I thought they might have said something to you, but I should have known they would keep my confidences. I appreciate them so much. Just wait until you move out. You'll see how great you have it at home."

Sierra thought she was going to be let in on some great secret, but all Tawni seemed to want to talk about was their parents. Sierra already knew she had great parents. That was not a secret. She drew the chopsticks back to her mouth, devoured her first bite of dinner, and answered Tawni with an "Ah-hmmm."

"I'm trying to make a big decision," Tawni went on. "I talked to Mom and Dad about it the other night, and of course I've talked to Jeremy about it endlessly, and my other friends. I'd like to hear your opinion before I take the next step."

"Ah-hmmm," Sierra answered again.

"Are you eating?" Tawni asked.

Sierra swallowed. "Boy am I! Sweet-and-sour pork. I got the last of it."

"Oh," Tawni moaned. "Don't tell me it's from that Chinese place downtown. I miss their egg rolls."

"Egg rolls," Sierra repeated, the suggestion sending her on a search through the rest of the bags and boxes. "No egg rolls, unless everyone else already got them. There's some rice left and some cashew chicken." Sierra stuck one of her chopsticks into the box and pulled out a chunk of chicken. "Oh, the chicken's good."

"Stop it!" Tawni practically screamed into the phone. "You're torturing me!"

"Then I guess we're even," Sierra said without thinking. "I've been tortured trying to figure out your big news."

Tawni paused and then blurted out, "I've found my birth mother. She lives in Reno. I'd like to meet her, but I don't know how to approach her."

Sierra plopped onto a stool at the counter. "How did you find her?"

"One of Jeremy's friends at school needed a project for his summer course in humanities. A bunch of us were sitting around one night, and I suddenly said, 'You can find out who my birth mother is and save me the price of a professional search.' He thought it was a great idea, and so I became his project."

Sierra waited for Tawni to go on. It seemed she wanted

the story to be drawn from her bit by bit. Sierra willingly coaxed out the next bit.

"What's her name?"

"Lina. Isn't that a pretty name? Lina Rasmussen."

"And she lives in Reno?" Sierra found her imagination suddenly flooded with images of a middle-aged showgirl who would be a gigantic disappointment to Tawni when she met her.

"She works at the university there," Tawni said, shattering Sierra's colorful image.

"What else do you know about her?"

"A few things," Tawni said slowly. "She was fifteen when she had me."

"Fifteen? Oh, man! Can you imagine? No wonder she gave you up for adoption."

Sierra regretted her flippant statement as soon as she made it. Tawni's adoption had always been a sensitive issue with her.

"I'm sorry," Sierra said quickly. "I didn't mean for that to sound that way."

"No, that's okay. Jeremy said about the same thing. He said that considering the alternative, he was really glad Lina gave me up for adoption."

"You mean, considering the alternative would have been an abortion?" As soon as Sierra said it, her hand flew to her mouth. "I did it again. I'm sorry, Tawni. Nothing I'm saying is coming out right. I'm just so shocked."

"Don't worry about it. You're completely right. Lina could have easily gotten an abortion, and I wouldn't be here today." There was a catch in Tawni's voice. "I guess that's why I wanted to find her. I want personally to thank her for choosing to give me life. I want her to know that her choice was the best one."

Tears flooded Sierra's eyes. "I think that will mean a lot to her."

"I know it doesn't always go well when an adopted child tries to make contact with her birth parents," Tawni said quickly. "One girl at work told me about a cousin of hers who found her birth father. She contacted him by phone, and he hung up on her. She wrote him a letter, and he never responded. I guess some people bury the memory so deeply they can't handle being reminded that they had a child."

"Are you going to call Lina or write her or what?"

"I'm not sure. That's why I wanted your opinion. I thought the next step would be clear after I talked with Mom and Dad, but they said it was up to me. Then Mom called back today and said she and Dad were split in their opinion. Dad thinks I should call her. Mom thinks I should write."

"And what do you think?"

"I don't know. Jeremy thinks I should just show up on her doorstep so she won't have the chance to hang up on me or not respond to my letter."

"That seems a little pushy," Sierra said. "I mean, how would you feel if you went through whatever she went through at 15, and then almost 20 years later, this person shows up on your doorstep?"

"Exactly. That's why I kind of like Mom's idea of a letter. That way I can say some of the things I really want to, like thanks for giving birth to me. That way if she's not comfortable responding, at least I've achieved my goal of telling her what I wanted."

"Do you think any of this bothers Mom or Dad?" Sierra asked.

"I don't know. At first they seemed pretty surprised but real supportive. You know how they are. Then today, I don't know. Some little things Mom said made me wonder if she's feeling strange about this, like she wants me to get it over with quickly."

"After all, she raised you," Sierra said.

"I know. That's why I'd never refer to Lina as being my 'real' mother. I'd only refer to her as my 'birth' mother. Mom is and always will be my real mother. I told her that."

Sierra adjusted her position on the stool. "Well, I know you've wanted to do this for a long time. I remember your telling me you were going to hire a lawyer. It looks as if maybe God is working things out."

"That's what it seems like to me," Tawni said. "Jeremy is probably more excited about this than I am. He says I need to solidify my identity."

"What does that mean?"

"That I need to become more secure in who I am and who God made me to be. I don't know what I think." Tawni sighed and went on. "Some people I know who are adopted say they rarely think about where they came from genetically. It's not been that way for me. It's bothered me for a long time. I want to see if I have her eyes. Maybe she would tell me I laugh just like my birth father. All the time I was growing up in this big family, people—complete strangers—would say things like, 'You don't look much like either of your parents.' Or I'd hear, 'All those Jensen kids sure resemble each other. All except the older daughter.' I guess it bothered me more than I ever realized."

"Yeah, but did you hear the rest of their comments?" Sierra asked. "They would say, 'That Tawni is much better looking than that younger daughter.' That's what I've had to live with. The shadow of the beautiful Tawni was a long one I couldn't get out from under."

Tawni sounded surprised. "Sierra! You of all people should know that we're not supposed to compare ourselves with others."

"Isn't that what you're doing?"

Tawni paused. "I guess maybe I am. This is what Jeremy has been telling me for a long time. That's what he meant by my solidifying my identity. Mentally, I know my self-image is supposed to be based in Christ, and I should be seeking to find out who God made me to be. But I guess I don't understand that yet in my heart."

Sierra nodded. She understood. It was wonderful having her sister open up to her like this. Neither of them spoke for a moment. Sierra took another bite of her dinner.

"Are you and Jeremy getting pretty serious about each other?" Sierra asked.

"Sometimes I think so. Other times I'm not so sure. He's never brought up the subject of marriage, if that's what you're asking. He's committed to finishing school, and he's committed to our friendship. We haven't opened up any other doors of possibilities. By the way, how are things going with Paul? You said a few weeks ago that he wrote you. Has he written again?"

"No. I wrote him twice and then decided to wait to hear from him before I contacted him again. It's hard to tell with guys, isn't it? You think they give you a green light, and then it turns yellow. You don't know if you should chance it and run through or hold back and assume that it will suddenly turn red on you."

Tawni gave a lighthearted laugh that came from a well of deep understanding. "You have it figured out, Sierra. That's exactly how it is with guys."

Sierra stared out the kitchen window. "I mean, I opened up my heart and told him things that I don't tell just anybody." She hadn't expected the tears that suddenly welled up in the corners of her eyes.

"And now you feel vulnerable," Tawni said. "You handed him your heart, and you're afraid he's going to tromp all over it."

Sierra sniffed. Her answer was a hoarse "Yes."

"It'll be okay," Tawni said quickly. "Even if he never writes you back, it's okay. Don't close up, Sierra. Don't lose that free-spirited exuberance of yours for any reason. Be yourself. Even if being yourself means you say or do things you regret. All relationships are a process. You'll learn as you go. We all do."

Sierra reached for a napkin from the basket at the end of the counter and wiped her eyes. "I wish I understood relationships better and that I had them figured out ahead of time." Sierra was thinking of Amy as well as of Paul. "If I knew what the other person was thinking or what that person was going through ahead of time, I'd know how to think and act and respond."

"Sorry," Tawni said. "It doesn't work like that. Sometimes all we can do is take the little bit of info we have and go with it. It makes you trust God absolutely."

"I guess that applies to Paul and me as much as it applies to your writing or calling your birth mom, doesn't it?"

There was silence on the other end of the line.

"You're right," Tawni said.

"All your friends and family are giving you the feeling it's a big green light to go ahead and call her, but then you find out it might suddenly turn red and you'll be breaking all the rules if you try to run it."

"Yes," Tawni answered quietly. "That's exactly what it is. I guess I have to take my own advice and go with the little bit of info I have. I have to trust God absolutely in this."

"So, how do you know if you did the right thing?" Sierra asked.

"I guess only time will tell."

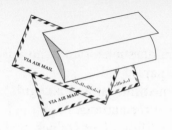

chapter six

*S*IERRA SPRINTED INTO HER LITERATURE CLASS JUST AS the bell rang. Mrs. Chambers gave her a friendly, scolding look. As Sierra sat down and took her notebook from her backpack, her heart was pounding. She was late because she had been talking to Amy in the hallway.

When Sierra had spotted Amy at her locker right before class, she had taken Tawni's advice and gone with what appeared to be a green light.

Sierra walked up to her friend and simply said, "Hi. Can we talk after school?"

Startled, Amy said, "Okay."

Sierra suggested they meet at her locker after school and that was that. She was trying to trust God absolutely, as Tawni had said.

"I'm handing out an assignment that is due on Friday," Mrs. Chambers said, passing papers down each row. "This is a list of American authors and the titles of some of their works. I want you to read and evaluate one of the works listed. If you would like extra credit, you may do two evaluations. The questions for you to answer are on the second piece of paper."

Sierra skimmed the list and recognized the names of only about half of the authors.

"Do not save this until ten o'clock on Thursday night," Mrs. Chambers said, perching on the edge of her desk. "You will need to go to the library and check out these books to read the sections listed. I have a few of the books in my library at the back of the room. You may check them out, but only until Friday."

Mrs. Chambers gave them a few minutes at the end of class in case they wanted to check out one of her books. Sierra took advantage of the opportunity and reached for a book of poems by Emily Dickinson. Vicki stood beside her and took a book by Henry Wadsworth Longfellow.

"Sierra," Vicki said, "I was wondering if you wanted to do something together sometime."

Sierra gave her a puzzled look. "What do you mean?"

Vicki's smooth cheeks began to flush. "I don't know. Go shopping or something."

Sierra tried to hide her surprise. "Sure. We could do that."

"How about today after school?"

"I already have plans for today."

"Tomorrow maybe?"

"I work tomorrow," Sierra said.

"Oh. Well, another time," Vicki said. "Let me know when you have some time."

"Okay," Sierra said. She looped her backpack over her shoulder and gave Vicki a suspicious look. *I didn't think she liked me. Is she trying to get to somebody through me? Who could it be? Randy?*

Sierra put away her suspicions about Vicki and spent the rest of the afternoon concentrating on what she was going to say to Amy after school. She had it all planned out and felt only a little nervous as she stood by her locker, waiting for Amy to show up.

Randy came by and said, "I gave my notice at the restaurant. Did I tell you already?"

"No. Did you give them two weeks' notice or what?"

"I offered two weeks, but he said I could be off at the end of this week if I worked the lunch shift on Saturday."

"What about your yard business?"

Randy shrugged. "I'll get somebody to help me."

Sierra noticed that his hair was back in a ponytail and tucked under his collar as if he were trying to hide it.

"What happened with the warning you got about your hair?" Sierra asked.

"Nothing."

"What are you going to do? Get it cut?"

"I don't know. Everyone was saying at lunch today that it's a dumb rule. They think I should petition to get the rule changed to say that if your hair is clean and neat, it doesn't matter what length it is."

"So you get to be the one to challenge the 50-year history of Royal Academy?"

Randy shrugged again. "I'm not exactly the rebel sort."

"Does everyone think you are because you're growing out your hair?"

"I grew it out for the band," Randy said. "I think it

gives us more of a connection with the kind of people who go to The Beet. What do you think?"

"I don't know. I haven't been to The Beet. And I haven't noticed the other guys' hair in the band. Are you sure you want to go to the wall on this one?"

Randy readjusted his backpack. "I don't know."

"Are you going to talk to your parents about it?" Sierra asked.

"I probably should."

Randy looked past Sierra and gave a chin-up greeting to someone behind her. "Hey, Amy. How's it going?"

"Hi, Randy," Amy said. Her dark eyes centered on Sierra.

"Hi," Sierra said.

"Well," Randy said, apparently reading the situation. "I'd better get going."

"That's okay," Amy said. "Don't leave on account of me. I just wanted to tell you, Sierra, that I forgot I have someplace I need to go this afternoon."

Sierra felt her heart sink. "How about later tonight?"

"I work tonight," Amy said. "And then I have a ton of homework."

"When would be a good time?" Sierra asked. "I really want to talk to you."

Amy smoothed back her dark, wavy hair. "I don't know." She smiled at Randy, not making eye contact with Sierra. "I need to get going. I'll see you guys." She hurriedly turned.

Sierra watched Amy practically run down the hall and out the double doors that led to the parking lot. A heavy

cloud of apprehension and frustration came over Sierra.
Randy must have seen it.

"Hey," he said, leaning over to make eye contact with
her. "You tried. Don't beat yourself up like this. Give it a
little more time."

"A little more time, huh?" Sierra said. "Why is it that
everything in life seems to require a little more time? I'm
tired of waiting! Why can't relationships move along
smoothly without all this . . . this . . . What is this?"

"Life." Randy looked serious. "This is life. It's nothing
like the brochure, is it?"

"I don't like it," Sierra said, giving him a pout. "Why
won't she just talk to me?"

Randy shrugged.

"It's so frustrating."

"I imagine it must be," Randy said.

Sierra sighed and readjusted the backpack slung over
her shoulder.

"Come on," Randy said, tugging on Sierra's sleeve. "I'll
buy you a taco and a milk. That'll cheer you right up."

Sierra pulled away. "Will you stop with the taco and
milk?"

"You're the only person I know who orders milk with
a taco."

"So?"

Randy led the way out of the school building. "I'm
buying," he said.

"Who's driving?" Sierra asked when they hit the parking lot.

"Me. My truck is over there."

They were on their way to Lotsa Tacos, which was only two blocks away, when Randy asked, "Did Mrs. Chambers give your class the same assignment we got?"

"Probably. We're supposed to read and evaluate one of the works of an American writer. Did you get one of the books from the back of the room?"

"No," Randy said. "Did you?"

"Yes."

"Do you think she would mind if we did our evaluations on the same author?" Randy asked.

"I don't know why not. I was planning to do mine tonight. I'll give you the book tomorrow. Make sure you turn the book back in on Friday because it's checked out in my name," Sierra said.

They decided to go inside Lotsa Tacos rather than drive through. Sierra brought her backpack with her and pulled out the Emily Dickinson book while Randy ordered their food. She skimmed the preface and flipped through the book, happy to see that all the poems were fairly short.

Randy returned with six tacos, a large soft drink, and a carton of milk.

"Didn't you have lunch?" Sierra asked.

"Yes. Why?"

"Never mind."

Randy sat down and motioned to the book. "Is that the book for lit class?"

"Yes." Sierra held it up for him to see. "Emily Dickinson. It's a collection of her poems."

"Poems?" Randy echoed. "I thought we were supposed to read short stories or something."

"Poems are better than short stories. They're images in a tiny box wrapped up real pretty."

"Terrific," Randy said, punching his straw on the table so the paper wrapper tore off. "I always wanted to do a report on pretty little images all in a row."

"Hey," Sierra said, quick to defend Emily's poems, "don't be like that. What about your music? When you write lyrics to a song, aren't you sort of writing a poem?"

"Hmmph," Randy said.

"Hmmph?"

"Yeah, hmmph. I don't know if I want to agree with you or not."

"Here, let me read you one. You might get some inspiration."

"Inspiration, huh?"

"Yes, listen to this. 'Out of the more than 1,700 poems Emily Dickinson wrote, less than a dozen were published during her lifetime. The first volume of her poetry was published four years after her death.' "

"When did she die?"

Sierra scanned the introduction. "I don't know. It says she was born in 1830." She felt a tinge of adventure, reading words that had been written more than a hundred years ago by a woman who had died never knowing she would be famous one day.

"Here, listen." Sierra leaned across the table and read,

> In lands I never saw, they say,
> Immortal Alps look down,
> Whose bonnets touch the firmament,

Whose sandals touch the town.
Meek at those everlasting feet
A myriad daisies play.
Which, sir, are you, and which am I,
Upon an August day?

"What is that supposed to mean?" Randy said, munching his taco.

Sierra felt her heart pick up its pace with a contented little jig. She knew what it meant to see those immortal Alps whose bonnets touch the firmament and sandals touch the town. She had picnicked last August in a field of daisies on those very slopes. Alex was the "sir" from her personal poetic picnic. And just like Emily, she had only soft questions about the roles she and Alex were to play.

Gazing out the window at the clear autumn sky, Sierra felt transported above the roar of the engines at the stoplight outside. She had opened her heart to Alex just a little last August, and it had proved to be an enriching, growing, and encouraging experience.

Suddenly, she felt okay about those two transparent letters she had written to Paul. Even if he never answered, she had grown from writing them. Maybe Paul was encouraged. That was what she wanted. Maybe in some relationships all the questions were never fully answered.

And maybe they didn't need to be.

chapter seven

"HELLO? SIERRA?" RANDY SAID, WAVING A hand in front of her face, blocking her gaze of the endless sky and bringing her thoughts back to the noisy fast-food restaurant. "Where did you go?"

She smiled but kept her answer to herself. "Should I read you another one of Emily's poems?"

"That depends. Will it send you on another trip?"

"I don't know," Sierra said. "Shall we live dangerously and find out?"

She turned to another page in the book and read,

> The way I read a letter's this:
> 'Tis first I lock the door,
> And push it with my fingers next,
> For transport it be sure.
>
> And then I go the furthest off
> To counteract a knock;
> Then draw my little letter forth
> And softly pick its lock.

There was more, but Randy interrupted her. This time he was the one looking out the window and apparently being transported to another world.

"Check it out!" Randy said. "That's the new turbo diesel 780. The black one there. They just came out. That's the first one I've seen."

Sierra glanced over her shoulder at the stream of cars. She had no idea which vehicle he was referring to, and she didn't much care. She was more interested in reading about this woman who knew what it was like to wait for a letter and then go hide away to "pick its lock" to fully savor it all alone. The image brought another smile to Sierra's lips.

"Are you going to eat that?" Randy nodded at her untouched taco.

"No, you can have it," she said, returning to her book and reading the rest of the poem to herself.

After Randy inhaled the taco, Sierra read another poem to herself.

"You know what?" she said to Randy. "I've changed my mind. You can't use this book. I think I'm going to have it for more than just tonight."

"You actually understand what she's trying to say?"

"No, not all of it. But parts of it apply to things that are interesting to me."

Randy wadded up the paper wrappers and carried the tray to the trash can without making a comment. Sierra followed him, carrying her still nearly full carton of milk.

"I'll get another book tomorrow," Randy said. "You can keep Emma all to yourself."

"Emily," she corrected him.

"Whatever," Randy said.

They climbed back into the truck and drove to the school parking lot.

Driving home, Sierra thought about the poems. She wondered if she could finish reading the whole book tonight and start on her report. It would be good to get a head start this semester. She was so captured by the three poems she had read that she wanted to slowly drink in the book before beginning her report.

Sierra parked in front of the house, and out of a habit she had developed recently, she opened the mailbox to fish out the stack of mail. Pulling open the screen door, she walked into the kitchen and plopped everything down on the counter.

"Hello!" Sierra called out. "I'm home."

"I'm down here," her mother called from the basement.

Sierra flipped through the mail, making a stack of bills and advertisements for her parents. There was a letter for Granna Mae and two other envelopes.

She suddenly stopped and held her breath. The two envelopes both bore her name and address, written in bold, black letters. The stamps in the top right corner showed a side portrait of the Queen of England. Each stamp had been canceled with a thick circle of ink and showed the date of September 12. The name in the top left-hand corner was the name she had repeated for months in her whispered prayers: Paul MacKenzie.

He didn't forget about me. These were mailed over a week ago. Paul has been thinking about me, too!

Sierra's heart was fluttering like a butterfly caught in a net. She couldn't stop smiling. No one was around to see her carefully lift the two letters and steal away to her favorite chair in the study.

Just like in the poem, Sierra closed the study's door and locked it. She pulled her chair over to where the late afternoon sun spilled through the French doors. There, in a spotlight of autumn glory, she sat down and held both letters, one in each hand.

Which one do I open first? Maybe Paul put the date on them on the inside.

Sliding her thumbnail under the flap, Sierra opened one of the letters and drew out the single, folded page of white onionskin paper. It crinkled when she lifted the two folds, revealing the familiar bold letters that came from Paul's hand. The date at the top was September 7.

Sierra didn't know if she could bear to open the next letter and leave this one unread. But it would make more sense to read them in order. She opened the second one more hurriedly. That three-page letter bore the date of September 10.

Pursing her lips together, Sierra went back to the first letter and read each word slowly.

Dear Sierra,

I haven't heard back from you, and I realize you may never write. As I said in my last letter, I would understand if you don't want to start up a correspondence.

Sierra looked up and spoke to the swirling stream of

dust specks riding on the afternoon shaft of light. "He didn't get my letters!"

She read on.

There is one more thing I wanted to say to you, and then I'll let you be. Months ago on the airplane you said something that has stuck with me. I wanted you to know. You asked how I felt now that my grandfather was gone. Do you know, you're the only one who ever asked me that? So many people tried to tell me how I should feel. They still do that here. They say, "Oh, you'll get on fine," or "You should feel proud to have been kin to such a man."

Sierra, only you asked how I felt. I wanted to thank you for that. It's given me some freedom to feel all the things I need to.

May the peace of Christ be upon you.
Paul

Sierra folded up the letter. She eagerly began to read the next letter.

Ah, dear Daffodil Queen,

Pulling the paper close, Sierra looked to the ceiling and bit her lower lip to stifle a giggle.

"Ah, dear Daffodil Queen," she repeated aloud. Paul had once seen her walking down the street in the rain with an armful of daffodils and had teased her about it. This time his title sounded sweet to her ears.

I have read and reread your two wonderful letters

at least half a dozen times, and they still make me smile. You have such a way with words. I could actually see some of the stories as you told them to me: your father taking you to the restaurant where your friends all worked and presenting you with the purity ring; Doug being chained to the Balboa Island ferry; and your surprise trip to Switzerland.

I laughed aloud when I read about how you and your friend knocked over the card rack inside that proper little shop in Basel. I know exactly what that's like. There's a tea shop my grandmother goes to every Wednesday and Saturday to meet her friends. She took me along my first week here, intending, I'm sure, to show me off to the dear women of the town so they could see if I was a suitable match for their granddaughters. We sat at a very small table by the window. As soon as the tea and biscuits were served, I accidentally kicked the leg of the decrepit table and brought the whole spread, china teapot and all, crashing to the floor.

Sierra tilted her head back and laughed. She could just see the little tea shop, since she had been in one in Ireland. She knew how serious the little ladies were about having a proper, quiet tea time.

Poor Paul. How embarrassing!

I began classes at the university several weeks ago, and now my life consists of books, books, and more books. Perhaps that's another reason I enjoyed your refreshing letters so much.

How was your first week of school? You said that you were having a misunderstanding with your friend

Amy. I've wondered how that all turned out.

Last year I had a lot of friends at school, and I always had someone I could do something with. Here, I have very few friends. I don't know if it's me or them. Last year I didn't have many friends who were what you would call a good influence on me. I haven't found anyone here who holds to the values I now embrace. So I spend a lot of time by myself rather than at the pubs with the others. It's actually been good for me. My grades are all high so far. I spend the weekends at my grandmother's, working around the place.

Have I told you about my grandmother's home? It's a cottage, really. The original foundation was laid something like 200 years ago. It's been renovated a dozen times. The most recent improvements were made about four years ago. My grandmother has a microwave and a new central, wood-burning stove for heat, but she'll never have a dishwasher or trash compactor. There are two acres of hilly, rocky land that have been in the family for generations. They used to keep sheep on the land, but now all Grandma keeps is a collie named Laddie and a small garden, which did poorly this summer because of the unusual heat.

I'm writing this on the train to Grandma's. My stop is the next one, so I'll bring this to a close. I'm already looking forward to your next letter. Perhaps there will be one waiting for me at the cottage. Please tell me everything that has been happening in Portland. Have the autumn rains begun yet? Or are you enjoying those brilliant blue skies and warm sunshine as the leaves begin their transformation? We've had very little rain here, but everyone is ready for the wet to return.

I send this with my prayers for you, Sierra. May the peace of Christ be upon you.

Paul

Sierra let the pages drift to her lap as the rhythm of her pulse slowed. The sunlight waltzed through the French doors warming her arms the way Paul's letter had just warmed her heart. She didn't want to move from this chair. She didn't want to lose this feeling. Ever.

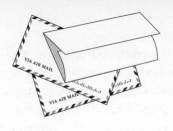

chapter eight

FOR THE TENTH TIME IN THE LAST FEW DAYS, SIERRA "picked the lock" on her wonderful letters from Paul as she sat in the quietness of her room to read them again. After she read them, she prayed for Paul as she had done many times. She prayed that God would make his path straight and that his heart would be responsive to all the things God was teaching him. It gave her comfort to know that even though they were so far away from each other in miles, they could be close in spirit. Paul was praying for her. He had said so.

Sierra had written Paul back right away Monday night after she had read his letters. It took her three hours to carefully craft her reply. She had given him her e-mail address and suggested they correspond by e-mail since it would be much quicker. Stopping at the post office Tuesday after school, she sent the long letter off by air mail. It would be hard to wait for his answer. If they could correspond through e-mail, they could chat on-line and answer each other the same day.

Now it was Wednesday evening, and Sierra had just

returned from the youth group Bible study at church. She went up to her room, where she shut the door and read her letters in private. There was something decisive and serious about Paul's handwriting. Each character was etched bold and black on the onionskin paper. Sierra noticed the way he crossed his T's with an upward stroke. This gave the whole page a feeling of optimism. The letters seemed to reflect Paul's personality as Sierra was beginning to know him: thoughtful yet hopeful.

"Sierra?" Her mom called out from behind Sierra's closed door. "Are you busy?"

"No. Come in."

Mrs. Jensen entered and sat on the edge of Tawni's bed. The top half of the bed was covered with a mound of unfolded clean clothes that Sierra had brought up from the laundry on Monday.

"I just talked to Tawni," her mother said.

Sierra nodded, waiting for her to go on. Before her mom came in, Sierra had folded Paul's letter and slipped it under her pillow, where she had kept his letters since the day she had received them.

"Tawni has decided to write a letter to her birth mother and wait for a reply. She wanted me to tell you what she finally decided."

Sierra nodded again. She was trying to read her mom's expression to see how she felt about all this. She appeared calm.

"How do you feel about all this?" Sierra asked. She felt a little strange, talking to her mom as an equal, asking about her feelings.

"I'll be honest. It disturbed me at first. There's so much that could happen or be said that could never be erased. Tawni has always been sensitive in certain areas. I was worried this would cut her deeply and leave quite a scar."

"It is kind of like venturing into the unknown," Sierra said.

"The more I've talked about it with your father and with Tawni, the more I think she's doing the right thing. This is a good step for her to take. I think the letter is a good idea."

"I do, too," Sierra agreed, leaning her elbow on her pillow and thinking of the hidden treasure under it. "Letters can really communicate a lot, can't they? I mean, you can go back and read a letter over and over and take your time to respond."

"You're right," her mom said. "I hope Tawni is prepared to never hear back, if that's what happens." She reached over and patted Sierra's leg. "The hardest thing for me is to realize you two are both old enough to make these kinds of life-affecting decisions."

"I think Tawni and I are both realizing that relationships can be complicated and there aren't always easy answers."

"That reminds me," Mrs. Jensen said. "Whatever happened with Amy?"

Sierra shook her head. "I don't think we're ever going to talk." She related what had happened at school on Monday and how Amy had made it clear she didn't want to discuss anything with Sierra. "It makes me feel awful," Sierra said. "Have you ever lost a friend like this?"

Her mom thought a minute. "Yes." She hesitated. "It's happened to me several times over the years. People change. Friendships change. I chose to take a different direction with a friendship when we moved here to Portland. I guess I was the Amy in that relationship. I simply didn't have the time or energy to keep in touch with this friend at the level she wanted. My life here is so different and in some ways more demanding than it was before. I'm afraid I hurt her feelings."

Sierra wondered if that was what was going on with Amy. Now that Amy was wrapped up in her relationship with Nathan, she didn't have the time or energy to keep a friendship going with Sierra.

After Sierra went to bed that night, she thought about Amy and the loss of their friendship. It wasn't even so much that Amy had a boyfriend. It was the way their friendship had ended. Sierra realized now, quite clearly, that she had a different set of values and goals for her own dating life. She had formulated what she called a creed, which outlined her standards in writing. She had assumed that Amy had the same set of values and that she would only go out with a strong Christian and would be deliberate about staying morally and physically pure. That didn't appear to be Amy's goal.

Before Sierra fell asleep, she wondered if she should write a letter to Amy. Her letters from Paul had meant so much to her. Tawni had decided to write a letter to her birth mother. Perhaps a letter would accomplish what Sierra wanted in making peace with Amy, even if they didn't remain good friends. Sierra knew it would have to be carefully written. As she lay in the silence of her dark bedroom, Sierra lined the words up in her mind, arranging and rearranging them like vowels and consonants in a game of Scrabble.

When she woke on Thursday morning, Sierra realized she had dreamed about her letter. In her dream she had handed the carefully written sheets to Amy in the school cafeteria, only to watch Amy drop them into the trash can, unread. As unsettling as the dream had been, Sierra still felt her idea was a good one. If only she could figure out what to say and the right way to say it.

There was no time to act on her idea that day because she worked after school and then helped serve dinner to the homeless who lined up at the Highland House. She didn't get home until after eight, and the first thing she did was go into the study and turn on her dad's computer. She checked the e-mail, just in case Paul had received her letter already and had written her back by e-mail. No messages waited for her.

Sierra opened a writing program and started to draft her letter to Amy: "Dear Amy, I want to tell you how sad I am that our friendship has gone on hold."

No, that didn't sound right. Deleting the line, she tried again.

Sierra kept reworking the letter, trying to express what she wanted to say without it sounding too strong. It was a lot harder than she had thought it would be. Her parents came into the study to say good night before they went to bed.

"A girl named Vicki called while you were at work,"

her mom said. "I left the note with her phone number upstairs on your bed."

"Thanks."

Her dad glanced at the computer screen. "Finishing up your homework?"

"I'm about to. I was just working on something else."

"Well, be sure to turn everything off when you go to bed." He patted her shoulder and gave her a quick kiss on the top of her head.

"I will," Sierra said.

She felt self-conscious about her words on the computer screen. They appeared so final there. Is that how they would seem to Amy? What if she tried her best to choose all the words so they sounded right to her, but somehow they didn't sound the same way to Amy?

Saving her efforts in a file marked "Amy," Sierra put away the letter and unzipped her backpack. The first book she pulled out was Emily Dickinson's poems.

"Oh, no!" Sierra groaned. She had forgotten about the writing assignment due the next day. With a glance at the clock, Sierra shook her head.

I can't believe I'm doing exactly what Mrs. Chambers said not to. I waited until ten o'clock on Thursday night.

Since schoolwork came easily for Sierra, over the years she had managed to get good grades with minimum effort. But now that she was beginning her senior year, it was important to her that she get straight A's. This last-minute effort with the poetry evaluation was not the way to start off in English.

When Sierra turned her paper in the next day, she asked

if she could do an additional report for extra credit.

Mrs. Chambers gave her a wistful look. "No, sorry. Next assignment maybe."

Sierra made a mental note: *No mercy from this teacher. Don't put off any assignments in this class.*

After class Sierra was returning the book to the library at the back of the room when Vicki came up beside her. Vicki waited until Sierra looked at her.

"Hi," Vicki said.

"Hi," Sierra echoed.

"I called yesterday when you were at work. I was wondering if you wanted to do something tonight."

Sierra looked Vicki in the eye. She wanted to say "Why?" but she managed to refrain and offered a smile instead.

"I thought maybe we could get something to eat or go to the movies. I didn't know if you were already doing something tonight."

"No."

Vicki smiled. "So what do you want to do?"

"Well . . ." Sierra shrugged. Then she heard herself say, "Why don't you come over to my house?"

chapter nine

"**W**HO'S COMING OVER?" MRS. JENSEN ASKED that evening.

Sierra was sitting on the floor in the family room going through the file drawer of all the videos.

"Vicki Navarone," Sierra said without looking up. "She goes to Royal Academy. Do you remember my saying anything about her before? She helped out at Highland House with Randy and me last spring."

"I remember your talking about Vicki, but I don't remember your saying you were friends."

Sierra looked up. "I didn't think we were." She turned her attention back to the videos. "I thought Tawni had all these in alphabetical order."

"She did when she lived here. I'm afraid no one has kept up the system."

The doorbell rang, and Sierra hopped up to answer it.

"That's Vicki. Are you sure it's okay if we watch a movie in here? The boys won't be crashing in on us, will they?"

"Gavin is over at Jason's, and I'll make sure Dillon stays upstairs. Have a good time."

Sierra felt apprehensive as she opened the front door. She never would have guessed that Vicki would have any of her Friday nights free, let alone want to spend one of them with Sierra.

"Hi. Come on in," Sierra said. "I was just going through our stack of videos to see if anything looked interesting."

"Sounds great! I love your house. That swing is so cute." Vicki had on a pair of shorts and a gray sweatshirt that said "Georgetown." Her silky, long hair was twisted up in a clip, and she didn't appear to have on any makeup.

"It's my grandma's house," Sierra said as Vicki entered and appreciatively glanced at the lighting fixture and wood trim in the entryway. "She lives with us, or rather, we live with her. Sometimes she gets kind of confused, so don't be surprised if she comes in and starts doing or saying things that don't make sense."

Vicki nodded.

They went into the family room, and Sierra returned to the video file, where she read off some of the titles.

"That sounds good," Vicki said as Sierra read. "I like that one. Oh, that's a great movie! I cried the first time I saw it."

Suddenly, Sierra stopped. This was all too unexplainable to her. Even though she knew she should think before she spoke, she didn't.

"Vicki, I have to ask you something. Why in the world are you here? I mean, why do you want to sit around my house and watch videos? I know you could be out with a whole lot of other people who have more exciting social lives than I do."

Vicki blushed.

"What exactly do you want?"

"I want to be your friend," Vicki said.

"Why?"

"Because I—"

"I mean," Sierra said quickly, trying to cover up her brashness, "we didn't exactly hit it off last year."

"I know," Vicki agreed.

"So what's changed?"

"Me," Vicki said without blinking. "I've been wanting to tell you . . ."

Sierra sat, attentively waiting.

"This summer I went to a church camp and I made a commitment to Christ. I've gone to church all my life, but I never realized I needed to surrender my life to God to have a relationship with Him. I became a Christian."

"You did? I mean, that's so great!" Sierra said. She felt like jumping up and hugging Vicki, but it still felt a little awkward between them.

Vicki smiled. "I can tell that God's been working in my life. He's been changing me, Sierra. On the inside. I don't want to hang out with the same people I used to spend time with. I don't want to get caught up in the whole party thing again. I want to stay strong in my walk with the Lord. That's why I wanted to get in with your group."

"My group?" Sierra held back the laugh she felt welling up inside. "I don't exactly have a group."

"I know that you, Randy, Tre, and some of the others from Randy's band are true Christians, and that's how I want to be, too."

Sierra lowered her head and shook it slowly. "Vicki," she said. The laughter in her throat had turned into an uncomfortable lump. "I feel really bad."

"Why?"

"I haven't exactly given you any reason to believe I am, as you say, a 'true Christian.' I mean, I am a Christian, and I feel the same way you do—I want to grow in my relationship with the Lord. But I've never treated you the way I should have, as a Christian. I'm sorry, Vicki."

"Don't be sorry," Vicki said quickly, reaching over to give Sierra's arm a squeeze. "I never treated you very nice, either. I knew you were different, though. You acted as though you were trusting in something or Someone bigger than yourself. You were what I wanted to be."

Sierra shook her head. "I have a long way to go."

"So do I."

There was a soft moment of quiet between them.

"I was hoping we could walk the long path together," Vicki said.

Sierra smiled. Vicki smiled back. It seemed their new friendship was somehow eternally sealed.

"Do you still want to watch one of these?" Sierra said, motioning to the stack of videos on the floor beside her.

"It's up to you," Vicki said.

"I'd rather talk," Sierra said, getting off the floor and settling on the couch across from Vicki. She tucked her bare feet underneath her and said, "Tell me about your summer. I want to hear about the camp and everything."

"I want to hear about your summer, too," Vicki said. "I heard you went to Europe."

"Just Switzerland," Sierra said, since "Europe" sounded so grand. "Well, and Germany. It was only for a week."

"Still!" Vicki said, opening her eyes wide. "I've always wanted to go to Europe. Anywhere in Europe. Did you buy a lot of souvenirs?"

Sierra laughed. "No. Can you believe it? About all I bought was some tea."

"Tea? I love tea."

"Do you want some now? Let's go in the kitchen."

The two friends talked and laughed over their cups of tea as if they had done this a hundred times together. The phone rang, and when no one else answered it, Sierra picked it up on the fourth ring.

"Hey, Sierra!" There was a lot of clanging of pots and pans in the background.

"Randy?"

"Yeah. Hey, Sierra, what are you doing tomorrow morning?"

"Working."

"What time do you go in?"

"Ten o'clock. Why?"

"I need some help. I have to be here at ten-thirty, and I couldn't find anyone else to do my lawns for me tomorrow. Can I hire you to help me mow lawns from seven o'clock to nine-thirty?"

"Hire me? You don't need to pay me. I'll help you. Where do you want me to meet you?"

"That depends." Randy hesitated.

Sierra looked at Vicki over her shoulder and raised her eyebrows as if to say, "Wait until you hear this one."

"That depends on what, Randy?" Sierra asked.

"Do you think you could use your father's lawn mower? If you can, I'll send you to the houses off of Hawthorne, and I'll do the others. There are only three lawns, and they're all close to your house."

"I think I know at least two of the houses," Sierra said. She had met Randy at his lawn jobs more than once. "Give me the addresses and tell me what to do. I'll be there."

"I owe you," Randy said gratefully.

"Oh, do I get to hold you to that?"

"Sure," he said. "How about if I drop off the addresses and the instructions on my way home from work tonight?"

"What time would that be?"

"I get off at ten o'clock. I'll leave the paper in the mailbox. Make sure you get started by at least seven-thirty, or you won't have time to finish."

"Got it," Sierra said.

"Oh, and hey, Sierra."

"Yeah?"

"Thanks again."

"Don't thank me yet, Randy. You don't know if I can do what your customers expect."

"Don't worry. These three yards aren't too complicated. Make sure you wear boots. I don't have workman's comp for my employees."

"You do offer vacation benefits, don't you?"

"Not for the kinds of vacations you go on."

In the background, Sierra heard someone call Randy's name.

"I have to go," Randy said. "I'll leave the paper in your mailbox."

"Okay. See you later."

Sierra hung up, and Vicki met her gaze. Her thin eyebrows arched up, silently questioning.

As Sierra stepped over to the counter where Vicki sat, an idea came to her. "Vicki, what are you doing tomorrow morning?"

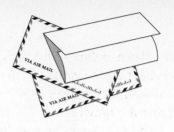

chapter ten

BY SEVEN-FIFTEEN THE NEXT MORNING, VICKI AND
Sierra were marching side by side up the street
to the first of Randy's lawn accounts. Sierra
pushed the mower like a baby carriage, hoping none of
their neighbors was up early enough to see their strange
parade. Sierra wore jeans, a long-sleeved denim shirt, her
dad's old cowboy boots, and a pair of stained, suede garden
gloves. Her hair was wrangled under a baseball cap. A
thick, curly ponytail hung out the back opening.

Vicki sported a sleeker landscaper's look. She wore
jeans, a short-sleeved knit shirt, and an expensive-looking
pair of sunglasses. Her hair was pulled back loosely in a
clip. She carried a pair of long-handled shrub clippers, a
rake, and a dozen black garbage bags.

"I've never mowed a lawn before," Vicki said with a
giggle. "I can't believe I agreed to do this with you."

"I'm beginning to wonder why I told Randy *I'd* do it,"
Sierra said. "I'm glad you came with me. It'll go a lot
quicker."

What Sierra didn't tell Vicki was that she had never

actually mowed a lawn before, either. Her brothers and father had always kept up the yard at home. While she had helped out plenty with the yard and garden over the years, she had never done the mowing.

"This is the first one," Sierra said, pulling the piece of paper from her pocket. She double-checked the address and read Randy's instructions aloud. "Mow front and back lawn. Small dog in backyard."

"Does that mean we're supposed to mow the small dog in the backyard?" Vicki said.

Sierra laughed. "Let's hope not."

"Should we start in the front or back?" Vicki asked.

"Front, I think. I'll start this thing, and we can take turns."

Sierra bent over the gas-powered lawn mower and gave the start cord a yank. To her amazement, it revved up immediately.

"Okay," Sierra said calmly as if she had done this dozens of times. "Here I go."

She pushed the mower straight up through the grass to the front steps. Turning around to go back the other way, she decided it would be more orderly to start on the other side of the yard. That way she could follow the line of the flower bed. To change her pattern, Sierra cut across the lawn in a huge diagonal and carefully followed the edge of the flower bed toward the house.

Vicki, who had been standing on the sidewalk watching, burst out laughing. "Look!" she shouted over the sound of the mower. "You made it look like Zorro was here." She motioned to the *Z* in the grass.

Sierra paused to see what she had done. In the spirit of the moment, she called out, "Watch this!" Then she made another long, diagonal line, crossing the first. "It's a bow tie," she called out over the roar of the lawn mower.

Vicki laughed and pointed at Sierra's masterpiece.

The front door of the house opened, and an older woman, wearing a long, green robe and moccasins, stepped onto the front porch. "What are you doing?" she shrieked.

Sierra bent to turn off the lawn mower. The only problem was, she had no idea how to make it stop. The mower rumbled on as she tried to answer the distressed woman.

"We're filling in for Randy," Sierra yelled.

"What?" the woman yelled back, her hands on her hips. It appeared she hadn't noticed the giant bow tie yet.

"I'll tell her," Vicki yelled to Sierra. She ran up to the porch and spoke with the woman.

Sierra fiddled with the mower, trying to stop the engine. Nothing worked. She could see the woman gesturing wildly with her hands as she talked to Vicki. Vicki hurried over to Sierra while the woman remained on the porch.

"She says we woke her up and that Randy doesn't do her lawn until after nine o'clock. She wants us to come back at nine."

"At nine! What about the bow tie?"

"I don't think she noticed it. Maybe if we leave really quick, she'll go back inside. Can't you turn off that noisy thing?"

Sierra shook her head. "I don't know how."

Vicki stared at her with disbelieving eyes. "We'd better

get out of here quick. Isn't the next house only a few doors down?"

"Yes, but what am I going to do with the mower? How do I get it there?"

Vicki shrugged. She glanced over her shoulder at the woman and offered a friendly wave, indicating they were on their way.

"Turn that thing off!" the woman yelled.

"Come on! Grab the clippers and stuff and let's go."

Sierra tipped the mower on the back two wheels and carted it off the woman's lawn. As fast as they could trot, the two mechanically challenged young women pushed the "live" mower down the sidewalk to the next house.

"Here," Sierra said, motioning for Vicki to grab the mower handle with her free hand. "Hold her steady."

Sierra slipped her hand into her back pocket and pulled out the instruction paper. She double-checked the address and jerked her thumb in the direction of the house they were to work on next.

"This one," she said loud enough for Vicki to hear over the rumble of the mower. "No dogs."

Vicki nodded and put down the gardening gear.

Sierra took the wild mower by the horns and forced it onto the tough grass. This time she carefully made her way up and down the perfectly square yard in tidy rows. Vicki went to work on the tall, spindly grass that sprouted at the sidewalk line. They both worked quickly, as if they were going to get caught and yelled at again. The front door never opened, nor did the front curtains part. If the tenants were home, they seemed unfazed.

Twenty-five minutes later, Sierra wiped the perspiration from her forehead and tried again to turn off the mower. It still wouldn't stop.

"It must be stuck," she yelled to Vicki. "We'd better go to the next house before it runs out of gas."

They trotted down the street looking like kids in a three-legged race. Both of them had one hand on the mower handle and carried garden tools in the other.

"Next block over," Sierra said, directing Vicki with a tilt of her chin. They turned left at the corner.

A man in jogging apparel came up the block toward them. A smile spread across his face. "Throttle stuck?" he hollered at them as he stopped jogging.

"I guess," Sierra called back.

"Mind if I have a look?" He bent down and began to fiddle with the contraption.

Sierra noticed more people were outside now. It made her feel as if they were becoming a neighborhood spectacle.

Why did I ever agree to do this for Randy? At least Vicki is being a really good sport. This would be much more embarrassing if I were by myself.

Suddenly, the motor stopped. Peace returned to the neighborhood.

"Thank you so much," Sierra said. "Do you think it will turn off okay if I start it again?"

"Let's try."

Their knight in shining running apparel gave the cord a yank, and the engine started its annoying rumble all over again. He then flipped back the lever on the handle, and it immediately stopped.

"Thank you so much," Vicki said, taking off her sunglasses to beam her appreciation at the man.

He took her praise and fixed his gaze on her face. Sierra didn't blame him. She had done the same thing when she had met Vicki. She guessed now it was something about the way Vicki's green eyes were framed by her thin, arched brows. It gave her a look of intrigue, like a smooth-skinned actress in an old spy movie. Sierra hadn't always admired the mysterious look. But since their long heart-to-heart talk last night, Vicki and her captivating looks didn't intimidate Sierra anymore.

"Hope it works for you," the man said with a nod.

He took off jogging again, and Sierra pushed the mower to the next house.

Vicki walked in step with Sierra and said, "Do you suppose he was our guardian angel?"

"Our what?"

"An angel of mercy sent to help us," Vicki said.

"In running shoes?"

Vicki laughed. "It's says something in the Bible about how we can entertain angels without knowing it. I read it a few nights ago in Hebrews."

"What are you saying?" Sierra asked. "You think that guy found us 'entertaining'?"

Vicki laughed again. "Maybe."

"Where does it say that?" Sierra asked.

"It's in the book of Hebrews. Somewhere in the last chapter."

"I'll have to look that one up," Sierra said.

"Where have you been reading?" Vicki asked. "In the

Bible, I mean. What part are you reading now?"

"I kind of skip around," Sierra said. "I was reading in the Old Testament, but when school started I began to read in Romans. I'm only about halfway through." It sounded more like a confession than an answer.

"You make it sound so bad," Vicki said. "I think it's great that you're halfway through. I mean, how many students at our school do you think even read the Bible on their own? And it's a Christian school. Don't ever apologize for reading the Bible, Sierra. No matter how fast or slow you're going through it."

"You're right," she said, pushing the mower onto the third lawn on their list. "I always want to read my Bible because I want to, not because I have to. It's my way of listening to God. I don't want it to be a duty. Do you know what I mean?"

Vicki nodded. She put the garden tools down on the sidewalk and tilted her head, giving Sierra a sunny grin. "You know what I've been doing?"

Sierra waited for Vicki to reveal her secret.

"I've been reading my Bible like it's a letter to me. I got the idea from my counselor at camp. I go in my room, shut the door, and read every word with my heart open. My counselor said to imagine that God, the One who knows me and loves me more than anyone else ever will, wrote those words just for me, because He did. That's what the Bible really is, isn't it? God's love letter to us?"

As Sierra watched, the morning sun peeked over the full elm tree behind her and sprinkled its amber blessing on Vicki's expectant face.

" 'Tis first I lock the door . . . then draw my little letter forth and softly pick its lock,' " Sierra recited in the golden, piercing moment.

"What?" Vicki asked.

Sierra smiled and shook away the Emily Dickinson quote. "I know what you're saying about reading letters and how that can be a wonderfully private time. God's love letter. I like that."

Vicki smiled back, her face aglow.

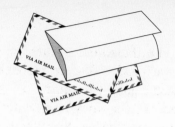

chapter eleven

SIERRA AND VICKI MANAGED TO FINISH THE SECOND lawn in plenty of time to return to the "bow tie" yard. When they got there, the woman was waiting on her front porch, dressed and wearing a scowl on her wrinkled face.

"What are you two trying to do?" she called as they headed up the walkway. "What did you do to my grass?"

"We're helping Randy out today," Sierra said, probably louder than she needed to. The way the woman was yelling, she appeared to have a hearing problem. Either that or she was really angry.

"I know that, but what have you done to my grass?"

The woman pointed at her yard. From the woman's perch on the porch, Sierra imagined the bow tie must have been quite evident.

"We're sorry," Sierra said, standing on the bottom step that led up to the porch. She didn't dare take another step forward. "We're going to fix it now. Then we'll mow the backyard. Is that okay with you?"

"Of course it's okay with me. That's what I pay for.

Make sure you clip those rose bushes on the side yard."
She seemed to eye Vicki with even more skepticism than
Sierra. "They need a good trimming."

Vicki nodded, and the woman came down the stairs to
direct Vicki to the rose bushes. Sierra started up the lawn
mower and went as fast and as precisely as she could across
the width of the lawn. Vicki and the woman hadn't
returned, so Sierra guessed that Vicki was receiving a
detailed lesson on rose-bush trimming.

When Sierra finished the front lawn, she headed for
the backyard. Vicki was patiently enduring the woman's
criticism, which she offered with each delicate clip Vicki
took of the massive climbing rose bush.

"Done already?" the woman asked Sierra.

Sierra tried to appear cheerful. "Yes. I'm ready to mow
your backyard. I think you'll be pleased with how the front
turned out. Should I go through this gate?"

The woman studied Sierra a moment. "You certainly
can't go through the middle of my house with that thing."

"No," Sierra said, swallowing her laughter, "I certainly
can't."

"Then go. Shoo." With a brisk flex of her wrist, the
woman dismissed Sierra and went back to inspecting
Vicki's work.

The backyard was very small. The dog, a black and
white mutt, appeared frightened of the mower and cowered
in his doghouse. Sierra mowed the lawn in less than 10
minutes, which was a good thing since she definitely
needed a shower before work and it was after nine o'clock.
However, the woman had other plans.

"Right here, next to the garden hose," the lady said to Sierra. "Those are weeds. If you don't pull them now, they'll be as big as my fist by next Saturday." She made a feeble fist with bony knuckles to prove her point.

Sierra picked at the tiny weeds.

"No, no, no! You have to pull them by the root, or they'll grow back. Go ahead. Dig down there. Get out the root."

Sierra did as she was told, bending and digging for almost half an hour all around the house. Wherever the woman spotted something growing that didn't meet her fancy, she yelled at Sierra, "There, right there. Don't you see it? Pick that out of there."

Vicki was still working on the rose bush. Every now and then the woman would call over her shoulder, "You are cutting those at an angle, aren't you?"

"Yes, ma'am," Vicki would answer patiently.

Finally, at nine-forty-five, Sierra stood up and said, "That's all for today. We really have to go now. I'm sure Randy can get whatever we missed next week."

The woman looked surprised. "Randy never does this for me," she said. "He only cuts the grass."

Sierra and Vicki exchanged pained expressions.

"That poor boy has two jobs, you know. He doesn't have time to weed my yard."

"Well, we would do more if we could, but I have another job, too, and I need to be there by ten o'clock." Sierra stretched her stiff neck from side to side and leaned back to remove the kinks from her spine.

"Well, then, go. Shoo!"

They gathered their things and headed down the street.

"Oh, and thank you, girls," the woman called out.

Sierra looked over her shoulder and saw the lady smiling at them. It was the first time Sierra had seen her smile all morning. She looked rather normal. Almost pleasant.

They hurried from the house, pushing the mower at top speed over the lines in the sidewalk. Clang, clank, clank, clang.

When they were a block away, Vicki said, "I know that verse in Hebrews said we're supposed to show kindness to all strangers, and we might be entertaining angels without knowing it. Even though I'm sure we entertained that woman thoroughly, I have serious doubts about her being an angel in disguise."

They both laughed.

"Could you believe it when she said Randy never has time to weed because the poor boy has two jobs?" Sierra said, huffing as she walked. "I should have started out by telling her I had two jobs, too."

"What time do you have to be at work?" Vicki asked.

"In two minutes."

"You're kidding. We should have left earlier," Vicki said.

"I know. But it was so hard to get away. She kept finding weeds that weren't even there!"

They ran up the driveway at Sierra's house, and she pushed the mower into the garage.

"I have to fly," Sierra said to Vicki. "Thanks so much for helping me. I couldn't have done it without you."

"It was fun," Vicki said. "I hope you have a good day at work. See you later."

Sierra was about to dash into the house. Then she stopped. Vicki was opening her car door.

"Hey," Sierra called out. "Vicki, I'll call you later."

Vicki waved and nodded. It all felt so natural. As if they had been close friends for years and did this every Saturday morning. The ease with which they had slipped into each other's lives amazed Sierra.

She didn't end up calling Vicki until Sunday afternoon. The answering machine picked up the call, so she left a message asking Vicki to phone her back.

The only call that came into the Jensen home for Sierra that evening was from Tawni.

"How are you doing?" Tawni asked her.

"Pretty good. I helped Randy mow lawns yesterday. That was an experience."

"I hope he paid you," Tawni said.

"No, it was a favor."

"You could never get me to mow anyone's lawn as a favor," Tawni said.

"This is how I see it," Sierra said, settling into her favorite chair in the study by the French doors. "One of these days I'll want Randy to do me a favor, and I'll use the opportunity to remind him of how I saved the day for him."

"What do you hear from Paul?" Tawni asked.

"I told you about the two letters I received on the same day, right?"

"You mentioned it the last time I called. That's why I asked. Did you write him back?"

"Of course. Right away. I sent him our e-mail address,

and I've checked every day. But he hasn't written back."

"Give it some time," Tawni said. "Did I tell you I wrote to Lina?"

"Mom said you were going to. What happened? Did you hear from her?"

"No, not yet. I know it's not the same thing as waiting to hear from Paul, but I do understand what you're feeling. Waiting is just awful. I keep thinking I should have said this or that differently. Once those words are on paper and out the door, there's no changing them."

"I know," Sierra agreed. "But with Lina, I'd think waiting to hear back from her would be much more nerve-wracking than my waiting to hear from Paul. What are you going to do if she doesn't respond?"

"I don't know yet."

"What if she writes or calls and asks you to meet her? Would you go?"

"Absolutely." Tawni paused and then said, "I've opened a new savings account just to be prepared to buy an airplane ticket in case she invites me to see her."

"You must be a nervous wreck."

"Sometimes I am. Most of the time I'm okay. A strange feeling comes over me every now and then. It's as if I really don't want to know what she's like. I don't want to see her. It's enough to know her name and make up my own image of her. Then, other times, I think I'd give anything to hear her voice or look into her eyes just once."

Sierra felt herself choking up. She had never fully understood her sister's feelings on any subject. Now, in a tiny way, she thought she understood what Tawni was saying. This whole issue was much larger for Tawni than Sierra had ever realized.

"I hope she calls you," Sierra said. "As a matter of fact, I'll start praying that she does."

"Thanks." Tawni's voice was warm and welcoming. "I appreciate that."

"Did you want to talk to Mom and Dad?"

"No, just tell them I called and that I got the job for the catalog shoot." Tawni's voice was flat.

"That's great! Don't they pay really well?"

"Yes."

"You don't sound very excited. What catalog is it?"

"It's a line of western wear. I don't remember the name. I get to spend four days wearing cowboy boots and forcing myself to smile beneath the brim of a cowboy hat. This will be a real stretch for me."

Sierra laughed. Even while they were growing up in a small mountain town near Lake Tahoe, Tawni never wore anything that looked country western, even when everyone else did. Now she was getting paid to dress up like a cowgirl.

"Don't worry," Sierra teased. "They'll probably play country-western music during the shoot to put you in the mood."

Tawni groaned. "If anyone ever tells you the modeling life is glamorous, don't believe them for one second. The torture we models must endure."

"Well, y'all would know, wouldn't ya, pardner?" Sierra teased.

"Right," Tawni said. "You should be the one in the

photo shoot. You and your beat-up cowboy boots."

"Hey, don't make fun of those poor ol' doggies. They served me well yesterday while I was mowing lawns."

"I'm so happy for you," Tawni said sarcastically.

It didn't carry the bite her sarcastic tone used to have when they shared a room and continually bickered at each other. This time it sounded funny, like one friend teasing another. It was nice.

The only problem was, at moments like this Sierra remembered her unsettled friendship with Amy and a sickening feeling returned to her stomach. She and Amy had once been able to tease each other and talk about the things they really cared about. Vicki seemed as if she was about to become that kind of friend, but how do people switch from one friend to another without any remorse?

After Sierra hung up the phone, she sat for a long time in the snug chair. She prayed for Tawni—that if it was what God wanted, Lina would call or write and that the two of them would be able to settle that relationship. Then she prayed for Amy. She guessed it was time to just let their broken relationship fade away.

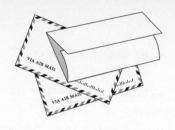

chapter twelve

"WHAT'S THE PLAN FOR FRIDAY?" RANDY asked.

He was stretched out on the school's grass during lunch. It had rained the day before, but today was clear and glorious. The autumn air felt crisp and cool. Bright orange sunshine came rushing at them, not directly overhead as it had in the summer, but at an angle. If Sierra had had a pair of sunglasses with her, she would have been wearing them.

"I don't know," Sierra said. "It's only Tuesday. Besides, I didn't know anything was planned. Is there a school football game or something?"

Sierra and Randy were joined by six other students who chose to eat outside rather than inside or to drive to a nearby fast-food place.

"The football game is an option," Randy said. "I was talking to Vicki, and she said she hung out at your house last Friday. Now that I don't work at the restaurant anymore, I thought we should all get together and do something."

"Sounds good to me," Sierra said. "Where is Vicki, anyhow?"

"I think she went to get something to eat with Drake and Megan."

Sierra took a bite from the apple she had brought with her that morning. An apple, a bag of onion-flavored potato chips, and a carton of cold milk—that was Sierra's idea of a perfect lunch. She considered asking if Drake, whom she had dated once, was now dating Megan. But Sierra knew better than to try to keep track of Drake's dating roster. All that mattered to her was that she wasn't on his list. Not at the top, not at the bottom. Not on the list at all.

Thinking of Drake's social life made her think of Amy. Sierra hadn't seen her yet this week. Amy had wanted to go out with Drake last spring and had tried to set up a casual date with him. She had included Sierra in the plans. They never did fix dinner for Drake and Randy the way Amy had tried to arrange. It hadn't been a big deal to Sierra, but it seemed to have been for Amy.

Sierra slowly chewed her bite of apple as the conversations swirled around her. She still felt bad. She had failed as a friend to Amy by not understanding what was important to her and working with her to help get some of those important things.

"By the way," Randy said, snitching a chip from Sierra's bag, "thanks for covering for me on Saturday. You and Vicki saved my skin."

"I'll remember that next time I need a favor. Believe me, it's hard work. My back was aching by the end of the day. It didn't help that I also mopped the floor at Mama Bear's."

"The weeding is what does it to you," Randy said, tipping Sierra's bag of chips upside down and shaking out the last few crumbs. "Mrs. Probst used to try to get me to weed for her. I did it once. Once was too much."

Sierra gave him a smirk. "It would have helped if you had warned me. She's the one with the dog in the backyard, right?"

Randy nodded.

"She got Vicki to trim her huge climbing rose bush, and she personally escorted me around the entire yard, pointing out everything she thought was a weed. Let me tell you, I pulled more green-tinged items from her flower bed than you even knew were there."

"You did?"

"Yes, and I was late for work because of it. All I can say is, it's a good thing Mrs. Kraus is so understanding."

"I guess this means if we do something Friday night, I have to pay for you."

"For Vicki and me," Sierra said. "Vicki worked her little fingers to the bone, too."

"Okay, McDonald's for both of you Friday night." Randy reached for his can of root beer and emptied it.

"McDonald's nothing! I'm thinking Tony Roma's. Don't ribs sound good to you?"

"Ribs, huh?" Randy didn't sound too thrilled about the idea of paying for three people at a place like Tony Roma's.

A tall senior named Tyler strode across the grass and joined their small group. He was the kind of guy Sierra considered to be conservative, studious, and a little on the shy side. This afternoon his countenance was far from subdued.

"Hey, Randy, I heard about the ultimatum on your hair. Way to go, man!"

Sierra looked at Randy for an explanation. His hair was still the way he had been wearing it since school started: long and pulled back in a ponytail.

"What happened?" Sierra asked.

Randy shrugged. "Nothing. I wrote a letter to the administration, that's all. They sent me a second notice, saying I had to get my hair cut, and I wrote them back explaining why I was growing it."

"He's not telling you the whole thing," Tyler said. Now everyone was listening. "Randy gave them an ultimatum."

"It wasn't an ultimatum. It was a letter."

Tyler jumped in. "The notice they gave him was the second warning about cutting his hair to codebook standards. If he doesn't do what they say by Friday, he could be expelled."

"Are you serious?" one of the other guys asked.

"My dad's on the board," Tyler said. "He was saying that they haven't had to deal with this kind of rebellion for years. There are always discipline problems, but not many acts of rebellion like this."

Randy shook his head, looking nothing like the rebel Tyler was making him out to be.

Tyler went on. "And since they decided not to change the school policy book, they're going to start coming down hard on any students who don't comply."

"Over the length of a person's hair?" Sierra asked. "What does that matter?"

"My dad says the issue is not the hair. It's the policy, because Royal students are supposed to set an example to the community," Tyler said.

Sierra looked at Randy. He was sitting back, taking it all in, seemingly unaffected.

"What did you say in your letter?" Sierra asked.

"I just gave them my reasons for having my hair like this, and then I told them it was up to them to decide. I said I'd go by their decision, whatever it was." Randy offered Sierra a crooked smile. "I gave them until Thursday to respond."

Tyler made a fist and raised it as if this were his battle. "You're the man, Randy! Way to go! Hit them with an ultimatum right back."

"I don't get it," Sierra said. "Why the ultimatums?"

She looked at Tyler, who had sat down next to her and was grinning from ear to ear. Sierra noticed that Tyler's hair was short and stubby on top, which wasn't especially attractive with his long face and broad forehead.

"It's the sheer brilliance of his response," Tyler said. "He's turning their big guns back on them. The revolution is coming!"

One of the girls in the group laughed and threw a wadded-up lunch bag at Tyler.

Sierra craned her neck and squinted against the afternoon sun to look more closely at Tyler. Why was he suddenly on this crusade? Did he have a battle of his own to fight with his father or with the board of directors?

"It's not that big of a deal," Randy said, leaning over and lowering his voice. "They sent me a notice at the beginning of school and quoted some rule in the handbook. So I read the whole handbook. There's a lot of stuff in there that doesn't seem to apply anymore. I pointed that out in a letter to them."

"Like what?"

"Like it says all students are supposed to stand during the morning flag salute, Bible reading, and prayer."

"What's wrong with that rule?" Sierra asked.

"Nothing. But when was the last time you had a first-period teacher who remembered to do the flag salute? Or read the Bible even once in class during the whole semester? And how many of your teachers pray before class?"

Sierra thought back. "Not many. I see what you mean."

"The handbook uses that verse in 1 Corinthians that says long hair is a disgrace to a man." Randy shrugged and went on. "I pointed out that in the community where I live, work, and hang out, my hair isn't considered long. It's only considered long here at school. Then I told them why I was growing my hair out. It's for the band. I quoted that verse in 1 Corinthians 9 in which Paul says since he's free from the law, he has willingly become all things to all men so that by all possible means, he might save some."

Sierra was astonished at Randy's calm demeanor as he stated his case.

"That's telling them," Tyler said enthusiastically. "Fight fire with fire. They don't have the right to go around dictating what we should do and wear."

Sierra could see who the real rebel was.

"Then," Randy concluded, "I told them about our mission statement for the band, which is to reach out to our peers on their own turf and communicate the good news of Christ to them. I said to effectively do that I believe I should wear my hair the way it is."

"That was it?" Sierra asked. "That was the whole letter?"

"And then the last paragraph."

"That was the ultimatum part?"

"I said I would willingly submit myself to their authority since they were the ruling body God has placed over me at this school. I said whatever they decided I'd abide by, but I needed to know by Thursday so I could comply with their previously stated deadline."

"And what if they tell you to cut your hair?" Sierra asked.

"Then I'll cut my hair."

"You don't care?"

"Not as much as everyone else seems to."

"If they make you cut it," Tyler said, "I think we should all cut our hair. We'll all get buzzes."

"Yeah, right," one of the other guys said sarcastically.

"I'm not cutting my hair," a girl named Bethany said. "It's taken me four years to get it this long."

"Exactly," Tyler said. "And that's why Randy shouldn't have to cut his, either."

Bethany pointed at Tyler. "You're the one who wants to fight this battle. Why don't you grow out your hair and see what your dad says?"

Tyler froze. Everyone waited for him to respond. "Like

that would ever happen," he muttered under his breath.

"I think Randy handled it really well," Sierra said. "Besides, aren't we supposed to be more concerned about what's on the inside of a person than about appearances?"

Before anyone could answer, the bell rang, signaling lunch was over. They rose as a group and returned to class, murmuring about the Thursday deadline. Sierra thought they looked like an unlikely band of rebels, especially with Randy as their reluctant leader.

"What do you think is going to happen?" Sierra asked Randy as they walked into class side by side.

Randy shrugged. His undaunted, easygoing grin appeared.

"Time will tell," he said.

chapter thirteen

*B*Y THE END OF SCHOOL ON WEDNESDAY, RANDY still hadn't heard the verdict regarding his hair from what Tyler was now calling the "PTB," or the "Powers That Be." Everyone at school seemed to know about it, and Sierra had noticed a group of students quizzing Randy at his locker before lunch. Randy didn't make it into the cafeteria, and Sierra wondered if he'd had a chance to eat at all.

After school she joined a dozen or so students who had gathered around Randy in the parking lot at the back of his truck.

"I think you should write them another letter," one of the girls said. "Tell them we all feel the same way. They shouldn't put such strong restrictions on us."

"Don't they trust us?" another girl said.

"We need a petition," one of the guys said.

A few more students gathered, and suddenly everyone seemed to be voicing opinions at once. Sierra was amazed at how calmly Randy was taking all this. He kept mentioning quietly that the PTB had until Thursday and this was only Wednesday. There was no need for radical action.

"Wait until tomorrow," he said. His steady voice carried over the ripples of murmurings from the students who seemed eager for a fight. "You guys seem to forget that I told them in my letter I would go by their decision, whatever it is. They're the authority over us here."

"Yeah, but what if their decisions are wrong? How can it be right to submit yourself to a bunch of leaders who are out of touch with reality?" The comment came from a short guy wearing glasses and looking startled that everyone had suddenly turned to look at him. "I mean, it only makes sense to go by their decision if it's a good one."

"That's right," another guy said. "We're the ones who are in touch with our culture. They are all way out of touch."

"They don't know what's really important," a girl chimed in. "We should be able to make our own rules as students and not have to go by their outdated laws."

"I think they should just let us all do what's right for each of us as individuals and only worry about our grades. That's why we go to school, isn't it?"

"My aunt said when she came here, they made all the girls wear dresses."

"Now that's discrimination! They can't do that anymore, can they?"

"I think they have to give students their rights now. And I say if we want the right to wear whatever we want or have our hair the way we want it, who are they to tell us what the rules are?"

"Yeah!" A common voice of agreement arose among

the 20 or so students who had now gathered.

"You guys," Sierra said, finally finding her voice, "this is so totally out of the book of Judges, I can't believe it!" She had enough steam for herself and Randy, since he had chosen to respond passively. "Don't you remember last year in Bible class? The last verse of the last chapter in Judges says, 'Every man did what was right in his own eyes.' That's why their nation fell apart."

"That was way back in Bible times," Tyler said, stepping forward and looking eager to debate. "What does that have to do with this situation? It doesn't apply at all."

"Oh, yes it does!" Sierra stated firmly, feeling her heart pound. "Everything God tried to teach them He still tries to teach us today. Can't you guys see that Randy is handling this the right way? He's willing to yield to the authority over him, but first he respectfully made his side known. We should all be supporting him, not trying to put him up as a cause for reform around here or something."

"Bravo," said a deep voice behind Sierra. She heard someone clapping and turned to see Drake, the star athlete, standing there with eight or nine people around him. "I'm on Sierra's side," he said, smiling at her.

"My side?" Sierra looked around at the crowd that had now grown to at least 30 students, almost all seniors. "There isn't a 'my side.' I'm just speaking up for Randy because everyone is trying to turn this into something it isn't."

"And as Randy said—" Bethany spoke up loud enough for everyone to hear. "There's nothing to debate until after the board makes their decision. And Randy plans to go by their decision, whatever that is. Why is everyone trying to turn this into a fight?"

"Let's meet here tomorrow after school," Tyler said. "Then we'll know if it's time we all started to take sides. It's way past time for some changes around here, and as I see it, this is only the beginning."

The murmuring started up again as the crowd slowly dispersed. Sierra could feel her heart still pounding. On impulse, she slugged Randy in the arm.

"What was that for?" he demanded, looking shocked that she would hit him.

"Why didn't you speak up for yourself?" Sierra challenged.

"Because I'm a pacifist. Unlike some other people I know," he said, rubbing the spot where she had clobbered him. "Ouch!"

"Sorry," Sierra said, forcing herself to calm down. "It just gets me that everyone is ready for a revolution, and they don't even know what they're fighting for. They're trying to make you their symbol or something. Doesn't that bother you at least a little bit?"

Randy shook his head. "It's like my mom always says, 'This, too, shall pass.'"

Sierra gave him a skeptical look.

"Relax, Sierra. They'll get over it. There's nothing to fight for. If the PTB say, 'Go to the barber,' I go to the barber. That will be the end of it."

"Somehow I have my doubts," Sierra said.

Vicki came up beside Sierra. "Hey guys, what's up? Someone in the hall said there was a meeting out here or something and to meet back here tomorrow."

"It's nothing," Randy said.

"It could end up being something," Sierra countered.

"We'll see," Randy said. "I have to go home and put some ice on my arm before it swells up."

"Somebody hit you?" Vicki said, looking first at Randy and then at Sierra.

"Yeah," Randy said dryly. "My campaign manager slugged me."

"I'm not your campaign manager."

"Okay, my own private crusader, then."

"I wouldn't have to crusade for you if you would fight your own cause."

"I don't have a cause, remember?"

Vicki stomped her foot on the asphalt. "Will somebody please tell me what is going on?"

"She hit me," Randy said, pointing at Sierra and sounding like a little boy. "And I'm going home to my mommy." His hurt, puppy dog look was awfully cute.

"Come on," Sierra said to Vicki while shaking her head at Randy. "I'll fill you in. Do you want to meet me at Eaton's Drugstore? I promised my mom I'd take Granna Mae there after school to get her out of the house for awhile."

"I have to go home," Vicki said. "I want to go to church youth group tonight, but my parents say I can only go out during the week if I have all my homework done, and I have a ton of it tonight."

"Then I'll see you at youth group, and I'll tell you everything," Sierra said.

"Okay, see you."

Sierra headed for her car at the other end of the lot. Randy revved up the motor of his truck when he passed her and gave her a broken wing wave as if she had maimed his arm for life. Sierra waved back. She felt foolish. Slugging Randy was something she would do to one of her older brothers. She hadn't even realized she had hit him until after she had done it. As much as she considered Randy her buddy, she had never hit him like that before.

"You know, Sierra Mae," she coached herself as she started the car and drove out of the school parking lot, "sometimes I think you're all grown up and sweet and mature, and then you get this ball of fire in you that explodes. When will you outgrow the feistiness?"

She was afraid she already knew the answer, and the answer was "Never." The Jensen family had a history of women who could hold their own in any situation and who never stopped feeling that ball of fire until the day they died.

Granna Mae used to be that way before her mind went fuzzy. Sierra remembered being in the car with her grandmother a few summers ago. They came to a stop sign in a residential area and saw two boys on the sidewalk contentedly eating Popsicles. An older boy on a skateboard came by, scooped up one boy's Popsicle, and took off down the street.

Granna Mae squealed the car's tires as she turned the corner in pursuit of the kid on the skateboard. The boy looked over his shoulder at her and tried to go faster, but he hit a rut in the sidewalk and took a tumble. Granna

Mae pulled the car to the curb, got out in a huff, grabbed the boy by his shirt, and gave him a vigorous scolding. The Popsicle had bitten the dust on the tumble, but Granna Mae extracted $1.12 in change from the culprit. She then drove back and delivered the money to the forlorn boy on the sidewalk.

As if that weren't enough, when the boys said they had bought the Popsicles from the ice cream truck, Granna Mae drove up and down seven streets before they heard the cranked-up music blaring from the truck. She then bought two ice cream sandwiches—one for herself and one for Sierra—and a new Popsicle, which she hand-delivered to the waiting victim.

There was no doubt the Jensen women fought for truth and justice. Years ago Sierra's mom had teased Granna Mae, saying all she needed was a bright red cape and she could get a full-time job protecting the world. Granna Mae had taken the teasing well. Sierra watched and learned because she had not always been so good-natured when her mom had teased her and said that she was just like Granna Mae. Sierra doubted that her mom had ever felt a ball of fire in her stomach, at least not of the same intensity as the fireballs that rolled around in the bellies of the Jensen women. For that reason and many others, Sierra felt tightly linked to her grandmother—even more than she did to her own mother.

Because of Granna Mae's spunky history, her feeble condition was frustrating to the whole family. They only knew her as strong, not weak.

Sierra could see how taking care of Granna Mae was

wearing on her mom. That's why Sierra had volunteered to help out in any way she could. So far the best and only plan she had come up with was to take Granna Mae out to some of her favorite places at least once a week. This afternoon the plan was to go to Eaton's Drugstore not far from their house. Eaton's had been in the neighborhood as long as Granna Mae had lived there. For more than 50 years, she had spent many hours at their lunch bar. It had been Granna Mae's tradition to take each of her own nine children to Eaton's after their first day of school and buy them chocolate malts. She continued the tradition with her grandchildren when they moved to Portland, but this year she didn't seem aware that school had started.

Sierra arrived home well past three-thirty, the time she usually got home. Her mother had Granna Mae all ready to go, and the two of them were waiting on the porch swing.

"Sorry I'm a little late. Are you ready to go to Eaton's for a malt, Granna Mae?"

She nodded. Her soft face was graced by a compliant expression. Sierra couldn't be sure if Granna Mae understood what was going on.

Mrs. Jensen gave Sierra an appreciative look and said, "Dinner won't be ready until six-thirty."

Sierra didn't know if that meant "Please take her and give me a break by staying away until six-thirty," or if her mother was merely giving Sierra a time reference on dinner.

"Okay," Sierra called back. "We'll be back by then." She wanted to make it sound as if they were going to have so much fun they would have to tear themselves away from Eaton's to make it home by six-thirty.

As Granna Mae lowered her thinning frame into the passenger seat of Sierra's car, Sierra wondered how much her dear grandmother was understanding today. Did she even know where they were going? Did it matter to her? Was this one of her bright days, and was she picking up every innuendo, including the one about not coming back until dinnertime?

The only way Sierra could know was if Granna Mae called her "Lovey." Only right now, as they drove down the street to Eaton's, Granna Mae wasn't saying anything.

chapter fourteen

*G*RANNA MAE AND SIERRA ENTERED THE SMALL drugstore and headed for the original Formica counter lunch bar. The red vinyl stools were exactly as Sierra remembered them as a child. Even the menu board above the long mirror didn't appear to have changed, except for the prices.

Sierra tilted her head and gave her companion a pleasant smile. "What do you think, Granna Mae? A chocolate malted, maybe?"

It startled Sierra to hear the tone of her own voice. She sounded like her grandmother. The tilt of the head and the inflection were exactly the way Granna Mae used to approach Sierra years ago.

What do you think, Sierra Mae? A chocolate malted, maybe?

Even that she said "malted" instead of "malt" was evidence of imitation of her grandmother. Something felt, oh, so strange. They had reversed roles. Now Sierra was the one driving the car to Eaton's and paying for the ice cream. Granna Mae had become the child.

"That would be lovely," Granna Mae said in response to Sierra's question.

For a moment, Sierra thought she said "Lovey," and she was about to feel relieved. But "lovely" was an altogether different word from Sierra's nickname of "Lovey."

"A chocolate malt, please," Sierra told the older woman behind the counter. "With two glasses."

"And a cup of coffee, please," Granna Mae ordered for herself.

Sierra smiled. "And one cup of coffee, please." It was hard to hold on to the image of her grandmother being a child if she was drinking a cup of coffee. Sierra was glad Granna Mae had ordered the coffee and that she had ordered it for herself. These were all good signs.

Sierra realized this was what her mother must go through every day as she kept an eye on Granna Mae. It was a constant guessing game. Is Granna Mae thinking clearly? What does she want? Can she ask for it herself? Will she be hurt or offended if I try to do something for her that she normally does for herself? Each of the clues Granna Mae sprinkled along the trail of the day had to be collected and analyzed. This could be an exhausting routine.

The door opened, and a little bell rang out its cheery chimes as a customer entered. Sierra glanced up. Her heart sprang into her throat. The customer was Amy.

Amy didn't see Sierra but headed straight for the pharmacy at the back of the store.

Until that moment, Sierra had been thinking it might be okay to let the friendship with Amy fade away. Now she suddenly felt differently. She remembered the time she had hidden in the basement as a child, waiting for someone to come find her. It struck her that perhaps Amy had pulled a trash can full of garden tools close to herself, in a manner of speaking. She was getting cold and cramped but wasn't willing to come out on her own.

I have to say something. But what? Maybe if I start talking, it'll come to me.

Sierra practically launched her tensed body from the stool as if there had been a spring on her seat.

"Granna Mae," she said slowly, "I'm going to the back of the store for a minute. If she serves you the chocolate malt before I get back, go ahead without me." Sierra realized she was speaking the way she would instruct a toddler, but she wanted to make it clear. "I'll be right back, okay?"

"Okay," Granna Mae said. "Don't rush yourself on account of me."

"Okay," Sierra agreed. She strode to the back of the store, moistening her dry lips and telling herself she shouldn't feel so shaken. This is what she had been wanting for weeks. Sure, it wasn't the best location for their talk, but it looked like the best she was going to get. She wanted to cry out, "Olly, Olly, Oxenfree" to signal Amy she could come out of hiding now.

"Amy, hi." The words tumbled out backward of how she had intended. "I was over at the counter with my Granna Mae when I saw you come in. How are you doing?"

Amy studied Sierra carefully. The expression on her face didn't change. She didn't even appear surprised to see Sierra. Her face held a flat, empty look.

"I'm fine. How are you?" Amy asked.

"Good. I haven't seen you at school all week."

Amy paused, looking at Sierra.

"I hope you haven't been sick or anything," Sierra said.

"No."

"Oh," Sierra said. "Good."

It was silent between them. No other customers were at the pharmacy window, and the pharmacist was in the back, apparently filling Amy's prescription. This was as good as it would probably get as far as a private spot for their long-overdue conversation.

"So," Sierra tried again, "how have you been?"

"Fine."

"Good."

Amy appeared reluctant to budge even an inch toward Sierra. Sierra knew she could always use dynamite words to break open Amy. At least that technique had worked in the past. Not today, though. This had to be done right. It was a delicate procedure, trying to gain back a lost friend.

"Have you been at school, and I just haven't seen you?" Sierra ventured.

Amy looked down and then back up, barely making eye contact with Sierra. "I don't go to Royal anymore."

"Oh. I didn't know. Why?"

Another pause.

"Is it because of your parents?" Sierra ventured carefully.

Amy nodded. She didn't look remorseful, nor did she look as though she was willing to share any more information.

"That's too bad."

"It's okay."

"Are things any better between your parents?"

"I guess so. In some ways. It's actually better now that they're not living together. They treat each other a lot nicer, and they both are trying to spend time with me. So it's okay."

Sierra was glad Amy was opening up a little. Taking advantage of the opportunity, Sierra said, "I'm sorry I wasn't home this summer while you were going through everything with your family. I tried to call from California, but I couldn't get hold of you. I left messages."

"You did?" Amy said.

"Yes, several times. Then I went to Switzerland, you know. But it was all so sudden I didn't have time to call anybody."

Amy nodded.

"When I came back, it was crazy getting ready for school, working, and everything. I tried waiting for you after work one night, but you had already gone. Then I showed up at your house that one morning with a picnic breakfast."

"When was that?" Amy asked.

"A couple of weeks ago. Didn't your dad tell you? I think I woke him up, so he wasn't exactly happy to answer the door."

"He didn't say anything," Amy said.

"Oh. I thought he would have. I brought breakfast over. I thought maybe we could talk."

"Look, Sierra," Amy said, putting one foot forward as

if trying to keep her balance. "I'm glad you're telling me this. I didn't know you had called me and come by. No one told me."

"I've been hoping we could talk. I don't like the way things are between us."

Amy stood a little stiffer. "I know you think we need to have this huge talk and get everything out in the open, but I don't feel that way. There are a lot of things better left unsaid. You have your life and your new group of friends and I have mine. Can we leave it at that?"

"I don't want to leave it at that," Sierra said stubbornly.

"Well, sorry, but you don't have much choice." Amy's dark eyes began to take on a spark of the old spirit. "I don't choose to be your friend anymore, Sierra. That's that."

"It doesn't have to be 'that,'" Sierra said, feeling lame as she said it. She urgently wanted to express what she still felt in her heart toward Amy.

Amy shook her head and looked away. "You have certain high expectations and goals that you force all your friends to live up to, and let's face it: I don't match up, do I?"

Sierra didn't know how to answer. She tried to choose her words carefully. Amy seemed like a rocket about to launch, and Sierra didn't want to be seared in the billowing white heat that would come with the takeoff.

Before she could decide what to say, the pharmacist stepped up to the window and called out, "DeGrassi?"

"Yes," Amy said, turning on her heel. "I don't have anything else to say to you, Sierra. Good-bye." Amy spoke the words firmly without looking back.

Sierra didn't know what to do. If she had been by herself and didn't have Granna Mae with her, the fighter in Sierra would have followed Amy out of the drugstore and into the parking lot, which would have been a much safer platform for potential rocket blasts. Sierra wasn't afraid of pursuing Amy, and she wasn't afraid of what Amy might say to her. At least it would be out in the open. But she couldn't leave Granna Mae alone any longer.

As Amy stood at the counter paying for her prescription, Sierra turned and went back to the lunch counter. So much for "Olly, Olly, Oxenfree."

Amy doesn't seem to be playing the game I thought she was. I figured she would be happy I kept after her until I "found" her. How could I have been so wrong?

Just as Sierra came to the end of the aisle that opened up to the soda fountain area, her heart stopped. There sat a chocolate malt in a silver container with two empty glasses. A cup of coffee rested on its saucer, still full. The two bar stools were vacant.

Granna Mae was gone.

chapter fifteen

"Granna Mae," Sierra called out, frantically glancing down each of the aisles. "Did you see which way my grandmother went?" she asked the woman at the counter.

"No, I didn't see her get up."

Sierra fled out the door into the parking lot. "Granna Mae!" she called out, not caring how silly she looked.

Amy exited the drugstore. When she noticed Sierra, she turned away and kept walking to her car.

"Amy, you have to help me. I've lost my grandmother!"

Amy paused and gave Sierra a skeptical look.

"She was with me at the soda fountain, but when I went back, she was gone. No one in there saw her leave. You have to help me find her. You know how she gets."

Amy hesitated and then let out a frustrated sigh. "Where do you think she went?"

"I have no idea."

"She's lived here almost all her life. She knows this neighborhood," Amy said. "Is there any place she likes to go? A park or something?"

"I don't think so. And if she's not thinking clearly, she could have wandered off anywhere and not known where she was. I think we should split up and drive around the blocks. That's what my mom and I have done before. Could you look on the next four or five blocks on that side?" Sierra said, pointing to the northwest side of the street. "I'll canvass this side."

"All right," Amy agreed.

"Meet back here after you've combed the blocks. And be sure to look in odd places like front porches and side yards."

"I'm not going to snoop in people's backyards," Amy said.

"Well, okay, but just call out for her. She knows you. She would get in the car with you if you asked her. Meet back here."

Sierra slid into her car and cranked the engine. Her heart was racing as she drove up and down the streets surrounding Eaton's Drugstore, calling out for her grandmother. "Yoo-hoo, Granna Mae!"

There was no sign of her anywhere.

This is awful, awful, awful! What am I going to do? I never should have left her alone. Not even for a minute. What am I going to do?

She canvassed the sixth block and still saw no sign of Granna Mae. Even on a good day, Granna Mae couldn't have made it much farther than this if she left the drugstore on foot. Still, Sierra drove down two more blocks, just in case.

Her search proved futile.

Maybe Amy found her. Oh, I hope Amy found her.

Sierra was in such a hurry to get back to the drugstore that she didn't look before making a turn at the corner and was nearly hit by a car that was going way too fast. She slammed on her brakes as the driver zoomed past her, giving her a dirty look as if she were the only one in the wrong.

Calm down. Getting yourself killed will not help the situation.

Forcing herself to be extra careful the rest of the way back to the drugstore, Sierra hoped and prayed with all her might she would turn into the parking lot and there would be Amy with Granna Mae in her car.

Amy's old beat-up Volvo was in the parking lot, but only Amy sat in the car. Sierra squeezed into a parking spot and hopped out of the car, running over to where Amy sat with her engine still running.

"I didn't see her," Amy reported. "I hope everything is okay. What are you going to do now?"

Sierra pounded her hand against the side of Amy's car door. She let out a fearful, frustrated sigh. "I guess I have to go home and tell my parents."

Amy pursed her lips together. "Well, I have to go, Sierra. I hope everything is okay."

"Thanks, Amy. Thanks for trying. I really appreciate it."

The two of them paused and made eye contact. No fireballs or flaming rockets traversed the space between them.

"That's okay. Bye."

"Bye," Sierra said reluctantly. She got back into her car.

On the way home, she decided to scan the neighborhood again, just in case either she or Amy had overlooked something.

What if Granna Mae went back to the drugstore?

Sierra turned around and headed for the drugstore. She hurried inside only to find the counter cleared. It was after five, and the fountain was closed. After walking up and down each of the four aisles, she asked the pharmacist if he had seen her grandmother. He hadn't. The woman who had been working at the front register had gone home, as had the woman who had been at the fountain. A high school student was now the cashier. She said she had been there for only 10 minutes, and she didn't remember seeing an older woman who fit Granna Mae's description.

"Thanks anyway," Sierra said. She forced herself to realize she needed to go home, tell her parents, and call the police. There was no way to describe the way she felt at that moment. All her life her parents had lectured her about being careless and misplacing important things, like her passport, for instance. How could she look at them and tell them she had misplaced Granna Mae?

Everything inside Sierra began to go numb, from her head down. The drive home seemed like the longest drive in the world. She barely felt the bump of the slightly raised curb as she pulled into the driveway. When she turned the keys in the ignition to shut off the car, she had no feeling in her fingers. If she would have slammed her foot in the door while closing it, she wondered if she would know it.

The sentences ran through her mind like a wild game

of crack the whip. Every sentence held her limp body at
the very end of it and snapped her back and forth with a
jolting force. She had felt nearly this bad once when she
was seven and had broken one of her mom's vases while
trying to get it out of the cupboard for a handful of wild-
flowers. She had swept up the pieces without getting cut
on the glass and kept it all in a grocery bag in the garage.
Then she waited until after dinner to tell her mom. That
was the most miserable dinner of her life.

Tonight there was no waiting until after dinner.

Sierra took the front steps two at a time, suddenly aware
that this wasn't about her failure or about her getting
punished for losing Granna Mae. This was about her
grandmother's safety, and the sooner she told her parents
and called the police, the better it would be for Granna
Mae.

"Mom!" Sierra cried out as she burst through the front
door. "Dad!"

"In here, Sierra," her mom called out calmly from the
living room.

"Mom, I—"

Sierra ran into the living room and stopped short.
There sat Granna Mae on the living room sofa, as large as
life and unharmed. Her mother sat on one side of Granna
Mae, and her dad on the other. All three of them looked
at Sierra with raised eyebrows, waiting for an explanation.

"Are you okay?" Sierra said, rushing to her grandmother and taking her hands. "What happened?"

"That's what we would like to know," her dad said.
"Mr. Svenhart brought her home."

"Mr. Svenhart? Why?" Sierra looked first at her father, then at Granna Mae, then at her mother for an explanation.

"He said she was sitting there all alone, and he was concerned." Mr. Jensen gave Sierra a stern look. "Where did you go? Granna Mae says you got up to go to the bathroom, and when you were gone such a long time, she went to the bathroom to check on you, but you weren't there. She waited at the counter, but you never came back."

Sierra slapped her forehead. "The bathroom," she muttered. "Of course. The only place I didn't look."

Mrs. Jensen leaned forward. "Sierra, this is serious. Where did you go?"

"I didn't go to the bathroom. I went to the back of the store, by the pharmacy. Only for a few minutes. I saw Amy, and I went back to talk to her. It seemed like it might be the only chance I'd have to get things right with her. We talked for just a few minutes, and then I went back to the counter, but Granna Mae was gone. Amy and I went in separate cars and drove all around the neighborhood searching for her."

Mr. Jensen looked upset. "Meanwhile, Granna Mae is sitting there, all by herself, at the counter for nearly an hour."

"I am so sorry," Sierra said, looking into Granna Mae's confused face and giving her hands a gentle squeeze. "I didn't mean to leave you like that. I thought you had left."

"Why would I leave? I thought you were having some difficulty in the bathroom. And then you were gone."

"I know. I'm sorry. I won't do that again."

"That's right," her mother said. "You won't do that again."

Her voice contained a frustrated edge. Sierra felt terrible. Here her mom had expected a few hours' break from Granna Mae, but instead Sierra had delivered a boatload of anxiety to all of them.

"I really am sorry," Sierra said.

She hated it when these kinds of things happened. It all seemed so innocent: a trip to the soda fountain, a chance to talk with Amy. And then it all turned around and bit her.

"Don't fret," Granna Mae said, letting go of Sierra's hand and stroking back a tendril of blonde hair from Sierra's grief-stricken face. "It's all over now, and we're all safe and sound."

"Would you like me to bring some dinner up to your room, Granna Mae?" Sierra asked. "Some soup, maybe?" She realized she was tilting her head and using the same voice she had used in the drugstore, the voice that mimicked the way Granna Mae had addressed Sierra when she was a child.

"That would be lovely." Granna Mae got up and excused herself to go up the stairs.

Sierra bit her lower lip. Again Granna Mae had used the word "lovely" when Sierra was so eager to hear the word "Lovey."

"This is much more serious than I think you realize," her mother said the minute Granna Mae was out of the room. "What were you thinking, Sierra?"

"It's like I told you. I saw Amy, and I thought I could

talk to her for a few minutes."

"You can't leave Granna Mae like that. Not even for a moment. You know that."

"I know. I was wrong. I'm sorry."

"Go easy on her," Sierra's dad said, patting his wife's arm. "Everything turned out okay."

"This time," her mom said. "What about next time?"

"We'll all make sure there isn't a next time," Mr. Jensen said, his voice calm and soothing.

Mrs. Jensen let out a deep, stored-up sigh. "If only it were that easy, Howard. You don't know what it's like." She got up and headed for the kitchen.

"What do you mean I don't know what it's like?" he asked, following her. "I live here, too. She's my mother. I know what it's like."

Sierra considered trailing along. Her impulse was to do things for her parents whenever she upset them, sort of a system of balances in which she did two helpful things to make up for her one colossal goof. However, it seemed better to stay back, at least for a few minutes, to let the two of them talk this through. She would wait five minutes or so and then make Granna Mae's soup. Soup was supposed to help whatever ails a person, right? What kind of soup could possibly make any of them feel better tonight?

chapter sixteen

*J*UST MINUTES AFTER HER MOM AND DAD HAD EXITED
the living room, the phone rang.

"Sierra, it's for you," Mrs. Jensen called out.

Joining her parents in the kitchen, Sierra took the portable phone from her mom and went over to the small, walk-in pantry in search of a can of soup.

"Hello?"

"Sierra, it's Amy."

Sierra stopped looking for soup and stood up straight. "Hi, Amy."

"I wanted to see if your grandmother is all right."

"Yes, she was here when I got home. A neighbor brought her back. You're never going to believe this, but she was in the bathroom while we were out looking for her."

There was a pause, and then Amy laughed. It sounded so good to hear her laugh again. "And you thought she was wandering the streets in a daze."

"I know. I didn't even think to look in the bathroom."

"Is she okay?"

"I think so." Sierra cupped her hands over the mouth-piece. "My parents are pretty upset, though." She could hear them still quietly "discussing" Granna Mae's condition at the kitchen counter.

Amy hesitated. "I just wanted to make sure your grandmother was all right."

"I appreciate your calling. Thanks."

"And I wanted to say that I appreciated your telling me that you tried to call and come over to see me. I didn't know that, and I guess I jumped to some conclusions."

Sierra closed the pantry door and pulled the chain on the overhead light. It was a tight squeeze, but Sierra didn't want to do anything to disrupt this moment she had waited for so long. "I've jumped to conclusions about you, too, and I know that wasn't fair."

"I meant what I said, though," Amy added quickly. "I don't want to sit down with you and have a huge discussion about my life."

"Okay."

"I'm not like you, Sierra. In some ways, we're similar and I think that's what first drew me to you last year. But I don't have all the same beliefs you do. I don't know if I ever did. I just tried to fit in, you know? And now I don't want to live with those kinds of expectations on me anymore."

"Amy—"

"Don't start in on me, Sierra. I'll hang up if you do."

"All I want to say is, okay," Sierra said quickly.

Amy didn't hang up.

Sierra kept talking. "Let's start from here. That's all I

wanted to say. I care about you, Amy, and I want to stay in touch. Whatever is comfortable for you is fine with me. I just don't want to feel that we're supposed to ignore each other because we've changed in the last few months. I've changed, too."

There was no response, but Sierra could hear Amy was still there.

"I can live with that."

"You know, Amy, I just thought of how you jumped in and helped me look for Granna Mae. Only a friend would do that. I guess you and I don't have to try to *be* friends. We just *are* friends."

"I'm not used to having friendships that keep going," Amy said. "I'm used to hanging out with someone and then going on and making new friends. So I'm not guaranteeing anything on my end to keep our friendship going. But I won't ignore you anymore, either."

Sierra felt as if a weight had been lifted off her.

"Maybe it's like you told me a long time ago," Sierra said, leaning against the pantry wall. "How did you say it? We're orbiting in different spheres, but every now and then our paths will cross. When they do, I want you to know that I'll be there for you the same way you were there for me today with Granna Mae."

"Thanks, Sierra." Amy's voice sounded tender. "I appreciate it. And I'll be there for you, as long as you don't have any expectations."

"I hope everything goes well for you at your new school."

"Thanks."

"Are you still working at your uncle's restaurant?"

"Yes."

"Maybe I'll run into you there sometime."

"Maybe."

"Well, call me anytime you're really bored. I'll probably be around."

"Okay. Thanks. I'll see you later."

"Bye, Amy." Sierra hung up, and leaning her head against the pantry wall, she let out a relieved sigh. It wasn't exactly the heart-to-heart conversation she had hoped to have with Amy, and it wasn't the outcome she had expected. But she was glad they had finally talked. Now she at least felt in some ways that the tension was settled.

What gnawed at Sierra were Amy's words about her beliefs. What did Amy mean when she said she didn't share Sierra's beliefs and maybe never really had? Did she mean Sierra's standards for dating? Or her beliefs in God? What was really going on inside Amy? Sierra knew she wasn't invited into Amy's heart, but at least she had limited "visitation rights." For now, she would be happy with that.

Opening the pantry door and stepping into the kitchen, Sierra found her parents were gone. Were they still discussing Granna Mae? Or was that conversation over and settled, the way Amy and Sierra had settled their conflict? Sierra guessed that everything had evened itself out for the time being. The next time something happened to Granna Mae, though, it was pretty certain the discussion would be opened again. That meant that more than ever Sierra needed to be on guard so she wasn't the one initiating any potential conflict over Granna Mae.

Sierra opened a can of minestrone soup, poured it into a pan, and began to prepare a dinner tray for Granna Mae.

"What a day," Sierra said to herself. She glanced at the clock and decided she'd better not plan to go to youth group tonight. Her mom would probably start dinner any moment, and Sierra knew it would be good if she helped out. That would leave no time for homework if she went to church, and she had a lot of it tonight. She remembered that Vicki was expecting her to be at church and decided she would call Vicki as soon as she delivered the dinner tray to Granna Mae.

The rest of the evening passed uneventfully, which was a good thing for Sierra. She helped with dinner and with the dishes. Everything seemed calm and back to normal with her parents and Granna Mae.

After eight o'clock Sierra lugged her backpack into the study with the intent of starting her homework. She turned on the computer and checked the e-mail. There were four for her dad, one for her mom from Sierra's brother Wesley, and two junk ads. Nothing from Paul.

Sierra wondered if her friend Christy Miller, who was going to school in Switzerland, had an e-mail address. Sierra had seen the computers in the library at Christy's school. Certainly, Christy could receive e-mail, if Sierra only knew where to send them. She had Christy's address and decided to write her a quick letter to get her e-mail address. It would mean sending another letter overseas and having to wait at least a week for the response.

Waiting was awful. It seemed terrible to have to wait days and weeks to hear from Paul. So much had happened already since she had written to him. Life was going by at the speed of, well . . . life. Her snail mail to Paul and his letters back weren't able to keep up the pace.

Sierra stopped typing her letter to Christy and stared out the window at the black night. *I wonder what Paul is doing right now. Is he at school? Studying? Going for a hike in the Highlands he seems to love so much? I wonder if he's thinking about me. And what would he be thinking?*

"Oh, Father God, I'm so glad You are everywhere at the same time. Would You please wrap Your invisible arms of love around Paul wherever he is, whatever he's doing. Let him know how much You love him and how much You care about everything that happens to him. Please direct him in his studies to do the best he can and to learn the things that will have value in the future. Prepare him for the work that You have designed for him. And keep him safe, Lord. Give him good friends, I pray, and excellent times with his grandmother. Strengthen him on the inside. Thank You, God, for hearing my prayers and for answering them in Your way and in Your time. I love You, God."

Sierra smiled to herself. She had prayed many months for Paul. In the beginning those prayers carried a different sort of emotion than what she felt now. Praying for Paul, fighting for him with her whispers to God, had been more an act of obedience. She did it because she felt the urgency to do so. Now that she and Paul were corresponding, it was different. His letters made her feel as if she had access to a little corner of his heart. That closeness made it a whole lot more fun to pray for him. A wonderfully calm, contented feeling came over her when she prayed for Paul.

It was amazing how a couple of letters could open up a relationship in such a warm way.

It reminded Sierra of how Vicki called the Bible God's love letter to her. *How would I relate to God if I didn't have His love letter to read? What would I think of Him? How would I talk to Him?*

Sierra stared out the window, pondering that thought. She had never considered that before. *Everything God wanted to say to me, He wrote down. And I can read it any time I want.*

The memory of the refugee children at the orphanage she and Christy had visited in Switzerland suddenly overwhelmed Sierra. *Have those children ever heard of the Bible? Has anyone ever told them how much Jesus loves them? How hard it must be for them to believe that after all they've been through.*

Quickly finishing her typed note to Christy, Sierra poured out her heart.

> It occurred to me that what you're doing in Switzerland, working with those children in that orphanage, well, it's God's work. I didn't see it when we were there. But tonight it seems so clear to me. If someone doesn't tell them about God, how will they come to believe in Him? And if they don't hear the Bible in their own language, how will they get to know Him? We have so much here in America, and I guess sometimes I forget that the rest of the world doesn't have the freedom or opportunity to sit down and just read the Bible whenever they want.

Sierra had to stop typing. The tears in her eyes made the computer screen go blurry before her. *Why didn't I ever realize this before? There are people all over the world who don't even have a copy of the Bible in their own language.*

It felt strange, being overwhelmed and so suddenly emotional like this. She had heard this kind of information from missionaries for years. She had even been on a missions trip and had visited the orphanage in Switzerland with Christy. Yet it had never hit her as it had in this moment: The Bible was God's love letter to the world, and there were people out there who had never received it, never read it.

Sierra pushed away from the desk and wiped her tears with the back of her hand. She hurried from the study and ran up the stairs to her room. It was a disastrous mess, as always. She knew where all her letters from Paul were. She had kept them in their original envelopes, and a few days ago had tied them with a black velvet ribbon that was part of a choker that broke. The letters were safely tucked under her pillow.

She checked, and they were all there, nice and flat.

Quickly scanning her room, rummaging through her dirty clothes, and kicking her shoes out of the way, Sierra searched for her Bible. She had read it two nights ago and had plopped it on the floor along with her science textbook. The floor, especially the floor in her room, was no place for such a treasure. She remembered how she had once crumpled up an early letter from Paul and tossed it aside in the same manner.

There the Bible was, peeking out from beneath a bath towel. Sierra snatched it up and held it close.

"I'll never do that again," she whispered.

Stepping over to the nightstand by her bed and clearing away the empty glass and the plate of cookie crumbs, Sierra placed her Bible next to the light.

All love letters are treasures and deserve a place of honor.

Feeling changed inside but not exactly sure why, Sierra went downstairs. She was determined to finish her homework as soon as she could so she wouldn't be too tired to read her Bible.

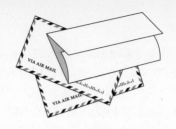

chapter seventeen

*T*HURSDAY AFTER SCHOOL, A LARGE GROUP OF STU-
dents gathered in the parking lot around Randy's
truck. Everyone was talking at once about what
was going to happen with Randy, his hair, and the administration's decision. It was all speculation because Randy
hadn't arrived yet.

"He's still in there with them," Tyler announced, jogging out to join the group. "They might be there for a long
time."

Sierra glanced at her watch. "I have to go to work," she
told Vicki. "Since I was late on Saturday, I can't be late
again."

"Do you want me to come by to tell you what happened?" Vicki asked.

"Would you?" Sierra said, giving her friend an appreciative smile. "That would be great. I'll see you then."

Sierra wedged her way through the crowd and hurried
to her car. When she had talked to Randy after lunch, he
had quietly told her he had been thinking about something
the leader had said at the youth group meeting the night

before. Randy didn't tell her what it was, only that the lesson was out of Romans 14. Sierra hadn't reached chapter 14 yet in her reading.

As she drove across town to Mama Bear's Bakery, she thought how blown out of proportion this whole incident seemed. What solution would please everyone?

She arrived at work a few minutes early, which was good because the place was unusually busy, and she was needed up front right away. Sierra went to work making special orders of coffees and lattes for the dozen or so women who flocked around the counter. They appeared to be some sort of group and very happy to be together. One of them had a chubby baby in her arms. All of them seemed to be speaking at once.

A tall woman with cinnamon-blonde hair and a gentle, curious gaze asked Sierra, "What is the difference with all your coffees? We don't have this where I am from."

"Oh. Where are you from?"

"I live in the Netherlands. There coffee is just coffee, not an experience, as it seems to be here."

She smiled, and Sierra smiled back as she went down the list and explained each of the items on the coffee menu.

The woman listened with care and then said, "I see. Well, I'd like a cup of coffee. Just coffee, black. Thank you."

Sierra poured the coffee from a fresh pot and handed the mug to the woman.

"How much is it, then?"

"Nothing. It's my treat," Sierra said. "Welcome to Oregon. I hope you have a good visit."

The woman's face lit up. "Thank you! How kind of you! Thank you."

She turned to join her friends at the tables they had pulled close, and Sierra took a dollar from her own pocket and put it in the cash register.

"Why did you do that?" Jody, her coworker, asked. "Now they'll all come up and want free coffee."

"You think so?" Sierra said. "I don't think so. If I can't offer a stranger a cup of cold water in Jesus' name, I can at least offer a cup of hot coffee, black."

Jody shook her head. "I don't know what you're talking about."

Sierra shrugged. "I felt like entertaining an angel."

Jody turned and walked toward the back of the shop, still shaking her head. "When I come back, I want you to start speaking English again."

Sierra wiped off the countertop with a warm, clean towel and smiled to herself as she listened to the group of women talking and laughing. It appeared to be some sort of reunion. The door of the bakery opened, and a petite, well-dressed woman stepped in. Immediately, squeals of joy rose from the group as several of the women hopped up to hurry over and greet her.

As Sierra watched these women, she thought about how valuable friendships are, friendships of every kind. She was so glad she had had a chance to talk with Amy. It was great that Sierra and Vicki were now spending time together. And Randy was the best buddy a girl could ask for. She loved having a friendship with Christy and her other older friends, who never treated her as though she was below them, even though she was younger. Then there were all the friends in Pineville she had grown up with. She hadn't kept in contact with them like she thought she would; yet she knew if she went back to her old hometown today, all her friends would be happy to see her, and they would pick up their friendships right where they had left off.

Now Paul . . . she thought of how to classify Paul. Was he a friend? A good friend? More than a friend? The strange thing was, she didn't feel that she needed to know. Not right now. Right now it was just what it was. Nothing more, nothing less. She had a wonderful, warm, encouraging correspondence going with a great guy, and that was all she needed to know.

Jody returned from the back with a tray of hot cinnamon rolls. Sierra drew in the tantalizing fragrance as she passed.

"I might just have to have one of those today," Sierra said. She went through spells when she didn't think she could eat another cinnamon roll since she was around them so much. But today it sounded like a good idea.

"Some of my friends might stop by later," Sierra said. "Would you mind if I took a break when they come?"

"Not at all. As long as you don't start passing out free cinnamon rolls to everyone."

"I won't. I paid for the coffee, you know."

"Yes, I saw." Jody pulled out the used coffee filter from the machine and motioned to the pot of steaming java. "Why don't you go offer them some free refills."

Sierra carried the pot over to the gathering of women and smiled. "More coffee for anyone?"

"Yes, thank you," said the woman from Holland.

A second woman held out her cup and asked, "Do you have any more cream? We used ours up."

Sierra was on her way to get a small pitcher of cream when the door opened and Randy and Vicki came in. Sierra turned, but when she saw them, she was so caught up in the hair issue that she called out a combination of "hair" and "Randy" and said, "Hey, Harry!"

One of the women at the table heard her and repeated loudly enough for her group to hear, "Harry! You guys, it's Harry!"

The women burst into laughter. All eyes were on Randy.

"I'm sorry," one of the younger women said. "It's a little joke for our group. Harry is our invisible hero."

Randy offered them a crooked grin and took the outburst in stride.

"You guys want something to eat?" Sierra said. "I'll be right with you."

She took the creamer to the table, and a woman with dark eyes said, "We're sorry if we embarrassed your friend. We get a little crazy when we're together."

"That's okay. He's not easily rattled."

Sierra returned to the counter where Jody had already served up a cinnamon roll for Randy and a pot of apple spice tea for Vicki. They went to a table at the front of the shop where Sierra joined them with her cinnamon roll and milk.

"I have a 15-minute break," Sierra said, tearing off a piece of roll and catching the drips of white frosting with her fingers. "So talk fast and tell me everything."

Randy gave his customary shrug. "I still don't know what I'm going to do."

"Didn't the PTB meet with you?" Sierra asked.

"They met with me, but they didn't give me an answer. They said my letter made them take a careful look at how some things were being done at the school. Then they said that since I handled it in such a responsible way, they would leave the decision up to me."

Sierra looked at Vicki, who nodded as if she were as amazed as Sierra. She knew how much Randy disliked it when his parents left important decisions up to him. He must be going through torture right now.

"You should have seen the mob in the parking lot," Vicki said. "They all acted as if it had been some great victory. They're sure Randy will not cut his hair."

"And you don't know if that's what you want to do?" Sierra ventured a guess, trying to read Randy's expression.

"I have to look at my reason. I told them it was so I would fit into my community and be accepted with the band and everything. But you know what? If you think about it, no one in the band cares. No one in my little community of musicians cares if my hair is short or long or if my head is shaved. It's only the administration at the school that cares. I don't think I have a very strong argument, really."

"Randy, they gave you freedom to do what you want," Vicki said. "I don't understand why you wouldn't just let it grow and be happy they saw your point."

"That's it, though. I don't know if I have a point."

"Now is a fine time to decide that." Sierra glanced at

the clock and felt annoyed that her break was already half over. "Can't you walk away from the whole thing and be done with it?"

"I don't know."

Vicki shook her head. "Some people think they should impeach the student body president and elect Randy. As they see it, he caused the board to break down and do things the way the students want them done by letting us make the choices."

"I don't want to make anybody stumble and fall over this. That's the verse from Romans I was telling you about, Sierra. Shawn talked about it last night."

"I remember that verse," Vicki chimed in.

"What was it?" Sierra was frustrated she didn't have the inside scoop on this verse they were talking about, but even more frustrated that she only had three minutes left to her break.

"It says something like 'Make every effort to do whatever leads to peace.'" Randy sighed. "Whatever I do, it should lead to peace and not more division at the school."

"I have to get back to work," Sierra said, pushing her barely eaten cinnamon roll in front of Randy. "You want the rest?" She stood and put her arm around Randy's shoulders. "I know you'll make the right decision."

Randy looked up at her and rippled his eyebrows with skepticism. "And how do you know that?"

"Because," Sierra said, her smile pouring over Randy like a blessing, "I'm going to be praying for you."

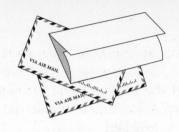

chapter eighteen

*S*IERRA PRAYED LONG AND HARD FOR RANDY ON Thursday night. She also studied for hours. When she was going over the material for her English test the next day, she came to a portion in the material about Emily Dickinson. She read it eagerly, hoping to know more about this woman who wrote the poem about the "immortal Alps" and "picking locks" on special letters. What she read startled her.

" 'As a child, Emily Dickinson attended the First Congregational Church of Amherst with her family. Of all her family, Emily alone resisted the revival that swept through the town in the mid–1800s. She stopped going to church sometime in her late twenties. Emily had few friends and kept to herself, spending nearly all of her 56 years at the Dickinson homestead.' "

Sierra looked up from her reading and felt sad. She knew from reading some of Emily's poems that she had a gentle reverence for God. She even had written about how God keeps His promises to sparrows and feeds them. She referred to Christ as "our Lord" and wrote of the love of Calvary.

So why had she stopped going to church? What had happened to her? What kind of friends did she have? Did they judge her or love her?

Sierra made a firm commitment that she would stick with Amy, no matter what. She wouldn't give up their friendship as if it were of no value to her. Her thoughts also turned to her friendship with Paul. Was Paul the kind of guy she would remain friends with no matter what? She hoped so. It was certainly that way with Randy. Why wouldn't it be that way with Paul?

Her homework wasn't finished until after ten. Sierra crawled into bed and eagerly opened to Romans 13. She wanted to get to chapter 14 where Randy said he had found the verse on trying to make every effort for peace.

Chapter 13 didn't end up being a quick read. The whole chapter was about having the right attitude toward those in authority over us. It all seemed to apply to the events of the past week, especially since Randy handled things so well by telling the board he would go by their final decision, whatever it was.

By the time Sierra had read through chapter 14, she understood why Randy was having a hard time deciding what to do. The chapter made it clear it wasn't always a matter of what was right for us as individuals. The test of love, the kind of love God calls us to show to others, includes being considerate of the weaknesses of others and what would be an obstacle for them in their walk with the Lord.

Sierra was so into the passage that she went on to chapter 15. When she reached verses five and six, she pulled out her pen and underlined them, reading aloud as she drew the straight line with the edge of her book marker.

" 'May the God who gives endurance and encouragement give you a spirit of unity among yourselves as you follow Christ Jesus, so that with one heart and mouth you may glorify the God and Father of our Lord Jesus Christ.' "

Even though it was nearly eleven o'clock, Sierra hopped out of bed and trotted to the phone in the hallway. She brought the phone back to her room, and sticking her cold feet under the covers, she dialed Randy's number. He answered on the second ring.

"Hi. Were you asleep?"

"I wish," he said.

"I found a verse. Listen, you have to hear this." Sierra carefully balanced the Bible on her upraised knees and followed the verse with her finger as she read.

"Did you get that part about the unity among yourselves?" Sierra asked. "That's what we need at our school. Not a revolution. We need to come together and be of one heart and one mouth. That's how we'll be an example in our community. We need a spirit of unity."

"Read the verse again."

Sierra read, and she could hear the pages flipping on Randy's side of the phone line.

"Sierra," Randy said slowly, "you're right. You're 1,000 percent right. Will you help me out tomorrow?"

"Sure. What do you want me to do?"

"Stand up in chapel and read that verse."

"What?"

"I agreed to say something in chapel tomorrow morning, since this has become such a big deal. But I'm not going to be there."

"What do you mean you're not going to be there?"

"I'll explain tomorrow. Just promise me that when you get to school you'll tell Mr. Ackermann I asked you to speak on my behalf, and I'll get there as soon as I can."

Randy, whose favorite word was "Whatever," had turned from complacent to wired in minutes. Sierra couldn't believe how excited he sounded.

"Would you mind giving me a little more information to work with here?"

"It'll make sense tomorrow. Trust me. Sierra, you're amazing. You'll never know how glad I am you called. Thanks a million. I owe you big time."

"Does this mean you're agreeing to pay for Tony Roma's tomorrow night for Vicki and me?"

Randy laughed. "Okay, okay. I'll pay. I'll see you at school." He hung up without saying good-bye.

Sierra held the receiver away from her and looked at it as if the beige piece of plastic had jilted her. "What was that supposed to mean?" she asked the silent phone. It did not answer.

The next morning before she left for school, Sierra tried to call Randy again, but his mom said he had already left.

"Oh, and Sierra," his mom added before Sierra could hang up, "thanks so much for your help. Randy said you gave him a verse last night that cleared everything up. You don't know how hard we've been praying."

"Can you tell me what's going on with him this morning?"

"I think he would prefer to tell you himself."

Sierra hurried to school. A dozen students were already inside the building, gathered around Randy's locker, apparently waiting to congratulate him for having broken through the rules of the PTB. One of the girls held a fistful of helium balloons. Sierra remembered the girl because she had worn a small silver ring in her pierced right eyebrow on the first day of school. The second day of school she wore two earrings there. The talk was that she had been sent home. Sierra didn't remember seeing the girl with earrings in her eyebrow since then. Today both earrings were back, and she was waiting expectantly for Randy, her new hero.

Even though Sierra felt like going over to Randy's locker and telling all of them he wasn't coming, or at least wouldn't be there until later, Sierra resisted the urge. They would only ask questions to which she had no answers.

First period went slowly. Chapel came right after first period, and Sierra hurried to get a seat near the front. She had talked to Mr. Ackermann, and everything was set. Vicki caught up with Sierra and sat beside her. The principal began chapel by asking the students to all stand for the flag salute. This had not been the habit, and everyone was surprised. He asked them to remain standing for the Scripture reading and for prayer. The freshman English teacher read from Psalm 8, and the football coach prayed. It was refreshing to see their teachers participate in chapel like that and lead the students spiritually. Sierra wished

Randy were here to see how the suggestions in his letter had made a powerful change already.

After some general announcements, the principal introduced one of the men on the school board. An elderly gentleman wearing a tweed jacket stepped up to the microphone.

"It's the PTB," Vicki whispered to Sierra.

"He doesn't look so threatening, does he?" Sierra whispered back.

"As most of you know, one of Royal's students has written a letter to our board this week. That letter has prompted much discussion. I must say, the discussion has been good. The board has decided to make one exception and to allow Randy Jenkins, for the benefit of his ministry, to keep his hair long. None of the rules in the student manual have changed, and no other student will be allowed this same privilege."

An immediate rumbling rose from the student body. Sierra felt that yucky feeling she had experienced in the parking lot when everyone was coming up with plans of what seemed right to him or her. It was as if a little ball of fire had ignited in the room, and she felt uncomfortable thinking about what might happen next.

The administrator continued. "I'm told that one of our students has something to say." He checked his notes. "Sierra Jensen, will you come up, please?"

Vicki reached over and gave Sierra's arm a squeeze. Sierra held her Bible with sweaty palms. As she stepped onto the stage, one of the students called out, "You tell 'em, Sierra. Equal rights for all of us."

The administrator stepped over to the microphone and loudly called the room to order. He motioned for Sierra to step forward.

Opening her Bible to Romans 15 and swallowing hard, Sierra addressed her peers. "Randy asked me to read this verse this morning. It's Romans 15:5–6. 'May the God who gives endurance and encouragement give you a spirit of unity among yourselves as you follow Christ Jesus, so that with one heart and mouth you may glorify the God and Father of our Lord Jesus Christ.' "

Sierra looked up at the sea of waiting faces. She had the microphone and felt she should give some explanation as to why last night at eleven o'clock it sounded like such a great idea to read this verse to the school. "You guys, we have to be united. The only thing that will show our community that we're true believers is if we have one heart and speak with one mouth rather than taking sides about things that only matter on the surface."

She had just finished the last two words when she saw Tyler rise in his seat. Before he could do or say anything, the back doors swung open, and someone came rushing in wearing a baseball cap. Sierra assumed it wasn't anyone from her school, since hats weren't allowed—another one of the frequently challenged rules in the student handbook.

The guy ran down the center aisle of the auditorium and walked up onto the stage. Not until he was next to her did she realize it was Randy. He wore a black baseball cap and from the back hung his blond ponytail.

When the student body realized it was Randy, they began to applaud, as if he had scored a glorious victory for all the wannabe individualists. Not only had he conquered the hair rule, but now he also was blatantly breaking the hat rule.

Sierra cast him a skeptical glance. The principal stepped onto the stage briskly and headed for the microphone.

Randy turned to Sierra and, with his crooked grin, said, "Watch this."

"Mr. Ackermann," Randy began. "Fellow students."

The principal marched over next to Randy at the podium. Sierra stepped back and then, deciding she was conspicuous, made her way down the three stairs and sat next to Vicki.

"What's he doing?" Vicki whispered. "What's with the hat?"

"I don't know," Sierra said. She suspected she was about to see her buddy do something crazy that would bring his new fan club to their feet with applause. If that happened, Randy could quite possibly be expelled from school.

"Don't do it, Randy," Sierra whispered under her breath. "Don't do anything you'll regret later."

"Did Sierra read that verse to you?" Randy asked, leaning too far into the microphone, causing it to feedback with a horrible squeal.

He leaned back. The principal stood right beside him, his hands folded in front of him, looking like a secret service agent.

Randy had everyone's attention, and so he began to speak. "I want you guys to know that the most important thing to me during this year at school is that we learn how to work together as a team. Like that verse says, we need to be one heart with a spirit of unity. I said in my letter to the board that I was growing my hair out so I could fit into the music community of Portland where my band plays, because that's my mission field. But the truth is, those people accept me exactly as I am, no matter how I look."

Sierra pursed her lips together and kept listening. Randy sure had everyone's undivided attention.

"This is my senior year," Randy went on. "Only one more year of my life will be spent here at Royal. Or actually, only nine more months. I want to thank Mr. Ackermann and the school board for granting me the freedom to choose what to do with my hair. And this is what I've decided."

With that, Randy ripped off the baseball cap and stood tall before a hushed crowd.

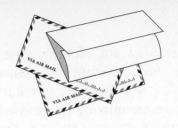

chapter nineteen

*S*IERRA'S MOUTH FELL OPEN IN SURPRISE. RANDY HAD cut his hair—short. It wasn't a severe, military-style short, but it was short. His ponytail had been cut off and was attached to the back of the baseball cap.

Randy waved the cap in the air and said, "I can wear this for concerts. For the next nine months of my life, I choose to go by the rules here at Royal and wear my hair like this." He leaned forward and used his left hand to rough up his inch-high hair. "What I want to say to you guys is unity. That's how people will know we're believers. Not by how we look, but by the way we act."

There was a pause, as if everyone was trying to evaluate Randy's actions and statements and decide whether to agree or not.

Sierra rose to her feet and began to applaud. She didn't care if anyone else joined her. Friends support friends, and right now she wanted everyone to know that she totally supported her buddy.

Vicki joined her. Then the rest of their row. Not everyone stood. Sierra noticed that Tyler didn't. Several guys were huddled together, murmuring and looking as if they were making fun of Randy for being so dramatic.

Mr. Ackermann stepped to the microphone, his expression showing his relief. "Thank you, Randy. You are a fine example of Christian maturity in a teenager."

Sierra heard that phrase used again after school, only this time it was said by two girls who stood across from Randy's locker.

"There's our school's fine example of Christian maturity," one of them said sarcastically.

"We were counting on you, Randy," the other girl said. "You let us down."

Sierra felt like tossing a smirk toward the girls and walking off. Randy went right over to them and started to talk with them, taking their verbal jabs in the face. It felt uncomfortable to Sierra to go over there now, since she would look like a snoop. So she went on to her locker and tried to figure out what books she needed for the weekend. Randy was still talking to them when she closed her locker door.

At lunch Randy, Vicki, and Sierra had decided they would meet at Sierra's at five-thirty, go out to dinner, and then go to the football game. Sierra didn't need to hang around to talk to Randy about anything else. Obviously, he wanted to keep the conversation going with those girls.

Sierra glanced over her shoulder at Randy one more time and then headed down the hall to the parking lot. Something gnawed at her. It was that verse. The part about the spirit of unity. She wasn't even trying to show unity with those girls.

Drawing in a breath of courage on the wings of a prayer, Sierra turned around, went back to Randy and the girls, and approached them with a smile.

"You're right," Sierra heard one of the girls say to Randy. "I know what you're saying, but people aren't like that. You can't tell people to be a team and think they're going to automatically do that."

"Hi," Sierra said, breaking in. "I'm Sierra."

"We know. We saw you up there today."

"I don't know your names," Sierra said, trying to sound genuine. Both the girls were new to the school this year, but Sierra hadn't paid much attention to them.

"I'm Tara, and this is Jen," the quieter one said.

"Are you guys going to the football game tonight?" Sierra asked.

They looked at each other.

"We hadn't thought about it," Jen said.

"We might go," Tara said hesitantly.

"We're going," Randy said. "I'll look for you and save some seats if you want to sit with us."

Tara smiled. "Thanks."

Jen offered a reluctant smile. "It's tough to be mad at a guy who's trying so hard to be nice." She reached over and rubbed his fuzzy scalp. "We'll see you later, Peach Head."

The girls turned to go and Sierra called out after them, "Bye. See you at the game." Then turning back to Randy she raised an eyebrow and said, "Peach Head?"

Randy shrugged. "I've heard worse today."

"Do you think anyone got the point? Didn't most people agree with you?"

"Yeah, most people agreed."

"So you think it's possible for our school to have some kind of unity?"

"I don't know," Randy said. "I hope so."

They walked together toward the parking lot, and Randy asked, "Is Vicki going to be at your house or meet us at Tony Roma's or what?"

"She's coming to my house. Remember? We'll see you there around five-thirty."

"Five-thirty," Randy repeated. "See you."

Sierra drove home thinking about how easy it had been to talk to Tara and Jen once Randy had broken the ice. And she never would have guessed that she and Vicki would have become such good friends. It made Sierra realize that if she started to take the initiative to make friends, this could be her best school year yet. And how fitting it would be, as Randy had said, to make their senior year one of unity in which the students worked together as a team. Maybe not everyone would want to make the effort, but Sierra knew she could. And she should. There was no reason she couldn't go out of her way to try to promote unity at school.

When she pulled into the driveway at home, her father was sitting on the swing on the front porch with Granna Mae beside him. It was a cool, pleasant October afternoon. A thin gray layer of clouds covered the sky, and a thick patchwork comforter covered Granna Mae's lap. Gavin and Dillon sat on an old rug on the porch playing a board game. Brutus, their big dog who thought he was part of the family, was tethered to the front pillar by a long rope. When he saw Sierra, he bounded toward her, barking and slobbering excitedly.

"Calm down, Brutus," Sierra said, slipping her hands behind his ears and roughing up his fur. "It's only me."

She held him by the collar and escorted him up the steps to the gathering on the porch. "What's going on?" she asked.

"Not much," Mr. Jensen said.

"Where's Mom?"

"She took the afternoon off," Gavin said. "We get pizza for dinner."

"She's doing some shopping," Mr. Jensen said, adding to Gavin's interpretation of the agreement Sierra had heard her parents make. One afternoon a week her dad would come home at noon so her mom could do whatever she wanted or needed to and not have to worry about Granna Mae. It meant her dad had to bring work home or work Saturday morning, but he had said that wouldn't be a problem.

"I'm supposed to remind you to check the oil in my car this weekend," Sierra said.

"That's right. Thanks for reminding me."

"And I'm going out to dinner with Vicki and Randy, and then we're going to the football game. I don't think I'll be home until after ten-thirty. Is that okay?"

"Call if you're going to be any later," her dad said. "Your curfew is eleven."

"I know," Sierra said. She reached over and squeezed

Granna Mae's hand. It felt warm. "How was your day, Granna Mae?"

She smiled at Sierra as if she didn't know who Sierra was or what she had just said. It tugged at Sierra's heart, but she forced herself to smile back at her grandmother. "I love you," she said and kissed the top of Granna Mae's soft, wrinkled hand.

"I love you, too," Granna Mae responded.

"I'm going to go change for tonight. I sure hope it doesn't rain." Sierra said.

"It's not supposed to," Mr. Jensen said. "The weather report was cloudy, but no rain until Sunday."

Sierra stepped over Gavin's outstretched legs and opened the front door. As soon as she went inside, the phone rang. She took off her backpack and picked up the remote phone in the kitchen. It was Tawni. The two of them chatted away like friends for 10 minutes. Sierra told her about Randy's bold move, and Tawni told Sierra about her western-wear photo shoot.

"If I ever hear another country-western song, I think I'll scream. They played that music all day."

Sierra laughed. "I told you they would."

She had been sitting at the kitchen counter but decided to take the phone into the study and turn on the computer to see if an e-mail from Paul might be waiting for her.

"All I can say is, the money is very good, and I'm thankful for the work."

"Did you hear back from Lina yet?" Sierra asked.

Tawni went quiet for a moment and then said, "No. And I think it's okay. Not that I've given up hope, but I think the important thing was that I got to say what I wanted to, which was thank you. If I was truly selfless, I wouldn't require a reply. But I'm not. Maybe someday she'll respond."

"I'm sure it must have been a shock to her," Sierra said, turning on the computer. "Give it some time. Maybe she needs a few weeks or something, to think all this through."

"I know," Tawni said. "I've thought of that. Believe me, I've thought of every possible angle. I don't have a problem waiting."

"Did you want to talk to Dad? Mom's not here."

"No, just tell them hi. I was doing my weekly check-in with the family."

"Do you miss us?" Sierra asked, grinning, knowing how her blunt questions always drove her sister crazy.

Tawni laughed. It was a cover-up kind of laugh. Then she said, "All right. Yes, I miss you guys. There. Now you know. Are you shocked?"

"No," Sierra said. "We miss you, too. I miss you."

A clumsy void of words followed their mutual confessions.

Tawni was the first to speak. "Well, I better hang up before I spend all my photo shoot money on this call."

"Say hi to Jeremy for me."

"I will. He's coming over tonight, and we're going out to dinner. I'm treating him to steak, now that I'm a rich woman."

"Sounds fun," Sierra said. "Talk to you later. Bye."

Tawni hung up, and Sierra scanned the computer screen, which showed all the retrieved e-mails. There were only two. Both for her dad from work. Nothing from Paul.

Sierra closed down the system and was about to leave the room when she decided to spend a few minutes in her favorite chair. It seemed a welcoming spot in which to feel sorry for herself. She noticed a picture on the seat of the chair. Looking closer, she realized it was a postcard. The picture was of a grand castle on a hill at sunrise. The sky behind the gray stone building was aqua blue with streaks of pink and mauve.

Sierra wondered who would send her dad such a postcard. Turning it over, she saw her name written in bold, black letters.

Sierra, she read.

> *Here's a pix of our famous Edinburgh Castle. I hope you can come to Scotland and see it one day. I'll write more this weekend but wanted to send this off to say thanks for the letter. It made me smile. Also, I don't think I'd like us to start e-mailing each other. There's something strong and enduring about old-fashioned letter writing. I like waiting for your letters.*
>
> *Time is our friend, Sierra. Let's enjoy the leisurely pace.*
>
> *Paul*

Sierra smiled as she turned the postcard over and studied the romantic shot of the castle. Then she read the card again. It was a good one. Not mushy. Not aloof. Just right. He had been thinking of her. He said he would write more later. And he said time was their friend. She liked that.

Paul was right. E-mail did bring with it an urgency and immediacy. Why rush?

She closed her eyes and held the postcard to her nose and lips as if she could draw in the fragrance of Paul's Scotland through the picture. She knew it was silly.

Sierra opened her eyes and looked around. How did the card end up in the chair? She could guess. Her dad, who knew her heart, must have been the one to pick up the mail this afternoon. He must have known that she would come here, to her favorite chair, and would find the postcard like a hidden treasure. The thought made her smile.

She rose and headed upstairs to put on warmer clothes and to tuck her postcard under her pillow. That was the only way to properly dream upon a castle. And that's where Edinburgh Castle belonged. In the "there" and "later."

Vicki would be here in a few minutes, and tonight Sierra would enjoy a fun evening with her friends of the "here" and "now." And the best part was, good ol' "Peach Head" Randy was buying.

Don't Miss These Captivating Stories in
THE SIERRA JENSEN SERIES

THE CHRISTY MILLER SERIES

If you've enjoyed reading about Sierra Jensen, you'll love reading about Sierra's friend Christy Miller.

#1 • Summer Promise
Christy spends the summer at the beach with her wealthy aunt and uncle. Will she do something she'll later regret?

#2 • A Whisper and a Wish
Christy is convinced that dreams do come true when her family moves to California and the cutest guy in school shows an interest in her.

#3 • Yours Forever
Fifteen-year-old Christy does everything in her power to win Todd's attention.

#4 • Surprise Endings
Christy tries out for cheerleader, learns a classmate is out to get her, and schedules two dates for the same night.

#5 • Island Dreamer
It's an incredible tropical adventure when Christy celebrates her sixteenth birthday on Maui.

#6 • A Heart Full of Hope
A dazzling dream date, a wonderful job, a great car. And lots of freedom! Christy has it all. Or does she?

#7 • True Friends
Christy sets out with the ski club and discovers the group is thinking of doing something more than hitting the slopes.

#8 • Starry Night
Christy is torn between going to the Rose Bowl Parade with her friends or on a surprise vacation with her family.

#9 • Seventeen Wishes
Christy is off to summer camp—as a counselor for a cabin of wild fifth-grade girls.

#10 • A Time to Cherish
A surprise houseboat trip! Her senior year! Lots of friends! Life couldn't be better for Christy until . . .

#11 • Sweet Dreams
Christy's dreams become reality when Todd finally opens his heart to her. But her relationship with her best friend goes downhill fast when Katie starts dating Michael, and Christy has doubts about their relationship.

#12 • A Promise Is Forever
On a European trip with her friends, Christy finds it difficult to keep her mind off Todd. Will God bring them back together?

FOCUS ON THE FAMILY®

£IKE THIS BOOK?

Then you'll love *Brio* magazine! Written especially for teen girls, it's packed each month with 32 pages on everything from fiction and faith to fashion, food . . . even guys! Best of all, it's all from a Christian perspective! But don't just take our word for it. Instead, see for yourself by requesting a complimentary copy.

Simply write Focus on the Family, Colorado Springs, CO 80995 (in Canada, write P.O. Box 9800, Stn. Terminal, Vancouver, B.C. V6B 4G3) and mention that you saw this offer in the back of this book. You may also call 1-800-232-6459 (in Canada, call 1-800-661-9800).

You may also visit our Web site (www.family.org) to learn more about the ministry or find out if there is a Focus on the Family office in your country.

▬   ▬   ▬

Chances are you'll like the "Nikki Sheridan" books, too! Based on a high-school junior named Nikki, whose life is turned upside down after one night's mistake, it's a series that deals with real issues teens today face.

Have you heard about our "Classic Collection"? It's packed with drama and outstanding stories like Louisa May Alcott's *Little Women*, which features the complete text—updated for easier reading—and fascinating facts about the author. Did you know that the Alcott's home was a stop on the Underground Railroad? It's true! And every "Classic" edition packs similar information.

Call Focus on the Family at the number above, or check out your local Christian bookstore.

Focus on the Family is an organization that is dedicated to helping you and your family establish lasting, loving relationships with each other and the Lord. It's why we exist! If we can assist you or your family in any way, please feel free to contact us. We'd love to hear from you!